For Andrew
Hox

A Summer in Mussel Shoals

ALLEN DIONNE

Books by Allen Dionne

FICTION
The Seeding Seven's Vision
The Seeding II Virgin Landfall
Duhcat, Mystery and Legend Unfold
A Summer in Mussel Shoals
The Seeding III Quest for Steel
Quest (Available August 2013)

Cover art: Allen Dionne, Copyright © 2013
Copyright © 2013 AD by Allen Dionne

Interior Book Design & Layout
www.integrativeink.com

My warmest thanks to: Stephanee Killen, Project Manager at Integrative Ink

ISBN: 978-0-9853979-3-7

A Summer in Mussel Shoals is entirely a work of fiction. Names, characters, places and incidents are a product of the Authors imagination and dreams. Any similarities to the real world are purely coincidental.

Printed in the United States of America by Lightning Source

*For Lana
Dearest*

Chapter 1

BOARDING THE DELTA flight out of Seattle, I was relieved that finally, in early middle age, I was able to afford flying first class, or business class as they now call it. I avoided the security lines full of families with bickering, pimply adolescents whose iPods and Gameboys seemed sewn permanently onto their fingertips, extensions of some modern technological wave of differential idealism.

They were not unlike the silent parents who glared at one another over the tops of their iPhones and Blackberrys, thinking of the damage packing had inflicted upon their already fragile relationships.

The kids would be in that relationship space soon enough, I thought. It never failed. Except for those rare occasions that we read about but have never personally experienced. You know the kind: married at the tender age of fourteen and dying at the ripe old age of ninety-six, both within three minutes of one another, while intertwined in each other's shriveled arms.

Enough of the cynicism. I'll attempt to move through my story without more, but I can't guarantee you a thing.

For me it was long hair—the idealism, I mean. That's what set me apart from my square parents. I had, until high school, a short cut done by my mother. She was too cheap to pay a barber for a decent job. Not that our family couldn't afford to have my hair professionally cut, I just think that she loved having me, at least once a month, under her complete and utter control.

"Grandpa is coming for a visit," she would say. No mention of my sweet, beloved and tender, cow-milking, school cafeteria-cooking, homemaker Grandma—who, since I was old enough to remember, nurtured me on her short visits with food, love, and all those understanding looks. Even if she had no idea what the seventies and long hair *really* meant, she didn't care about all that. She just loved seeing us grandkids no matter what we looked like.

Grandpa was different. Only the redneck rough and tumble logger and high climber was mentioned by my mother, as if he were a legitimate reason to butcher my hair—hair that had just begun to grow out from my mother's last foray into scissorsville.

His idea of fun was sheer torture to a young city boy: Indian wrist burns, knuckle grinds when he shook hands, the infamous knuckle scalp burn, which in modern times has been affectionately renamed the noogy. Most likely this was the least painful of his deviated and assorted shows of masculine affection, cloaked as grandfatherly love, but which I came to realize many years after he was gone were only violence subdued into something loggers, living without women in isolated camps for weeks at a time, considered affection.

Anyway, at fifteen—with the family psychologist seeing each of us children separately once a week, and then the family in group once a week—after several years of begging to grow my blonde hair long, I finally had an ally.

Her name was Virginia. An old—well...at that time anything over forty was ancient—single, chain-smoking shrink, who in my private sessions would just sit and stare at me, lighting one cigarette after another from the previous smoldering butt.

I often wondered what went through her mind in those private silent sessions. But she did say it wouldn't hurt for me to grow my hair long. Mom consented.

So in my book, Virginia was all right, if not slightly disturbing to a horny fifteen-year-old. I mean, each drag she took off her cigarette was exhaled with such a show of enjoyment, it looked to *me* like she had just finished a very satisfactory orgasm.

I never desired to get into Virginia's head or bed. I just want to thank that nicotine-stained woman for setting me free. No longer was I identified with the rednecks! I was a full-blown longhair, and reveling in my new status amongst kids my age who had shunned me before.

Hell, my hair hadn't been growing out more than three weeks when I got offered my first toke of pot. Next came the long-anticipated invitation to my first kegger.

Life was good, in a very simplistic way. That one small, hard fought and lengthily desperate battle won had catapulted me into a new and glorious life. And *that* life had brought me onto this airplane nearly thirty years later, and the story I'm beginning to share with you.

With the long hair grew an intense love of rock 'n' roll and rhythm 'n' blues. Naturally some of the Southern bands like Lynyrd Skynyrd, Alabama, and others were on my favorite playlist. Yet I had never heard of Mussel Shoals, Alabama—the town where most of that music was originally recorded—until much later in my life, long after I had cut my prized tresses.

For me, this trip was both a long deserved vacation and some well-earned quiet time to write a freelance piece I had longed to do for years. A publication called *Rolling Stone* had accepted my idea to do a history piece centered on the rise and fall of the great '60s and early '70s southern rock bands. I was their chosen author.

The title I was thinking of was something like, "The Rise and Demise of Something-or-Other..." I'm still working on that. I'm waiting for a bit of inspiration to rain down from the heavens and land in my brain.

Although, when it comes to inspired writing, I have been experiencing a three-month drought.

Believe it or not, I have not been a successful writer for very long. Good fortune hovered over me for a brief moment. I got some good reviews on a couple of novels that I had eeked out in my not-so-available spare time while working a real job sixty hours a week, and bang! I was hit in the nose with more book sales than I had dreamed of in my most optimistic moments.

Somehow or another, I had managed to hit the knuckleball of life and a home run at the same time.

Being on a constant, grueling promotional tour for nearly a year, I had become burned out. I was becoming more and more cynical by the minute. I mean, more cynical than I normally am. I was also completely out of ideas for a new novel.

Something kept niggling the back of my mind, the absurd idea that I could write a piece based on truth instead of completely make believe. I poured some mental fertilizer on the idea, and that all brings me up to this page in the story.

You see, the *idea* is to go to Mussel Shoals, to interview people who were there in the Day. I would attempt to get a different perspective on the bands, the recording studios, and how the massive wave that has long since receded affected everyday life in a little old town in northern Alabama.

Chapter 2

THE COMMUTER PLANE landed. Taxying down the runway, the airport seemed so small I thought I was seeing an old war movie where the plane is forced to land at an abandoned airstrip. As we rolled up near the shabby little building that stated proudly, "Mussel Shoals International airport," I wondered at the absurdity. What famous people had this airport seen in the past? What stories could it tell? How long had it been since it had hosted an international flight?

The door of the plane opened, and a wave of humidity hit me like stepping into a hundred and ten-degree sauna for the first time. I could barely breathe. Maybe I shouldn't have come in summer, I thought. Perspiration began to run down my back and into my butt-crack.

Great! I was going to look just like those southern farmers you see in the movies: walking around with giant brown wet spots exuding from some of the most sacred parts of my body.

There were no cabs waiting, so I asked the guy sitting next to me about it.

"Taxicab?" he said, and gave me a look like I was obviously from New York City. "None too many of 'em around hea'. You could call and wait. Might be a spell."

I considered asking just how long a spell *was* in Mussel Shoals, but thought better of it.

"Wife's pickin' me up. We could drop you in town if you don' wanna wait."

Now, my mother always taught me *never* to ride with strangers. This guy talked a little funny, but he really didn't seem strange. I was desperate, and said, "That would be wonderful."

Then I asked if his car had air conditioning.

"Ain't no car, issa pickup." And he laughed good-naturedly. He didn't answer my question about the air, so I just assumed I shouldn't expect it. When the ride came, it was like something George C. Scott had driven in the movie *The Flim-Flam Man*.

There was a passel full of kids up front. At least I think they call them a passel down here. The man kissed his wife through the window, then walked around to the other side and climbed in.

I didn't want to appear as one of those dumb city slickers by asking where I was riding. I threw my two, new, beautiful pieces of luggage in the back and climbed aboard. I was a bit dismayed to find one of them had landed smack dab on top of something resembling excrement, but I sure didn't believe it could be, so I just held on and concentrated on seeing the sights.

What a sight it was to see. I don't think I have ever seen so many rusty tin roofs in all my life. There were tin roofs on shanty shacks and warehouses, on doghouses, and a lot of people houses as well. These people were real fond of tin, I soon realized.

The man hadn't asked where I was going. The truck just stopped in the middle of a bunch of old stores, many with boards on the windows. I heard him say, "Well, this is downtown. You have a good trip now, ya hea'!"

That was my cue to disembark. I wasted no time in doing so. As the truck left me in a cloud of noxious black smoke, I would for years to come swear that I had heard the old time actor Walter Brennan cackling somewhere in the background.

I saw the Motel sign a couple of blocks away, so I started walking toward it. The Internet said it had a pool and air conditioning, so I was making my way to it like a man dying of thirst in a barren desert. The problem was just that. I *was* dying of thirst after about twenty...well, maybe it was only ten paces. Flying always dehydrates me, and I had read stories of what happens when a person develops sunstroke. Not pretty, so I figured I'd better get out of the beating rays immediately.

Ahhh! I spotted what I had been searching for. It wasn't one of those cool, easy to see, lighted signs, so I almost missed it. It said BEER, and it was painted in canary yellow on a piece of old plywood standing up inside a window that looked like it hadn't been washed since "Sweet Home Alabama" had been played hourly on most radio stations America-wide in the early seventies.

I drug myself and my bags through the door, expecting as you would, that a bar would be cool inside, and have some patrons, too. *So much for expectations*, I thought

Behind the bar was one of the biggest black men I have ever seen. I mean he wasn't the tallest, but he was *really* big.

Sidling up to the bar, which was made of rough shipping pallets covered on top with some more of that old plywood, I sat. I immediately felt something poking my hamstring and looked down to see that the stool was made the same way. A bent nail had been pounded down almost all the way, and the head was scratching me. I tried to ignore the nail and chalked it up to atmosphere.

He looked at me and didn't say a word. *Not the friendly type*, I thought. No wonder business was slow. You see, I pride myself on being able to walk into nearly any commercial establishment and pick up on the reasons it is doing well, or poorly, at once. This place was *screaming* at me.

"I'd like a beer…please." I had looked at him closely, and then added the please as an afterthought. The Big man didn't look friendly, so I figured a little charm couldn't hurt.

He reached under the plywood and brought up a can. Now, I don't normally drink beer from cans. This one said, "Beer" in great big letters. It had no brewery name on it. I was sure he wasn't attempting to pass off an imitation, but I'd never seen beer like that before. Even if I had, it surely wouldn't have been my choice. I'm a micro-brew kind of guy. So I asked him what other kinds he had.

I will remember his first spoken words 'til my dying day. They so surprised me that I was speechless for a full five seconds, which was a first for me. His voice was deep and had a strange…shrill edge to it, like he was offended or something. And I was trying *very* hard *not* to offend him! As I said before, he was *really* Big.

"Ain't no utha!"

Now, I don't consider myself to be slow on the draw mentally, but this time anyone observing would have guessed differently.

"Okay…" I said masterfully.

He slid the can to me and said, "Six bits."

I had heard the term "two bits" when I was a kid. Some old timers used to say that…but six bits? It took my heat-stressed mind a moment to calculate.

He just glared. It seemed like *that* can of beer was the only one left in the whole wide world, and he didn't *want* to sell it to me.

Now I know cheap beer goes for about three bucks a six-pack. So this guy was clearing about a quarter on my transaction. Looking around the place and estimating his average traffic flow, I quickly calculated his monthly business income, before things like rent, air conditioning, and refrigeration. He was obviously cutting some corners there. His inflow was about three hundred seventy-five dollars. I had no idea what rent in this neighborhood was, but felt it would have to be conservative. So I guessed his net monthly was running about ninety bucks.

I wasn't going to ask him to start a tab. His scowl told me he wasn't really the trusting type. I opened my wallet, then glanced behind me nonchalantly to see that no one was there looking into my travel stash before I pulled out a twenty. I slid it across the bar to him and picked up the can. It was room temperature. "Do you have a cold one?" I asked.

He didn't say anything for another uncomfortable five or six seconds, then he shoved the bill back to me, and I got the message loud and clear. There was only *one* kind of beer here, and it came warm.

I thought his gesture meant he wanted me to leave, but he spoke up, relieving me of that somewhat astounding thought.

"Got anythin' smaller?" he asked.

I dug frantically in my pockets for loose change, then remembered my habit of shedding all my loose change before I go through airport security. I hate that buzzer and the looks people give you when you *finally* pull an errant penny from some unknown pocket you had completely forgotten about.

I must have had that deer in the headlights look I can get when I'm lost at a crossroads and am locked up in fear.

He pulled my twenty back, turned, and walked away from me, shaking that big wide neck. Well, it really looked more like three big truck inner tubes, stacked one on top of the other, not a neck at all. Maybe that's not the right analogy, but at the time…maybe the heat was getting to me…it looked just like three huge, stacked inner tubes.

I opened the beer, grimacing while he had his back turned, and slugged down about half the can. The carbonation burned my throat like other beer when you drink it that fast. It was wet. I was thirsty. By the time he had wrangled a table of decrepit old men playing checkers for proper change, I had the beer finished.

He counted out my change very professionally, laying it on the counter. I asked if I could trouble him for another. He looked at my pile of change, calculating quickly I could see, whether my purchase would force him to walk anywhere to make change for a second time. Satisfied, I could tell by the merest hint of a smile at one corner of his mouth, he said, "No trouble."

This time the deep voice had no shrill edge, and he pulled another can from under the bar—if you could call it a bar.

The room seemed to be getting hotter. Or maybe it was the pressure I had felt when he silently glared at me. Anyway, the next can actually felt a tad cooler than my hand. I opened it quickly and chugged down about a third of it.

"See, 'tain't ha'f bad when you open your throat like that," he said, smiling. The man had the whitest teeth you could imagine. They were perfectly aligned, and I knew instinctively that he had been born with the genes that made teeth like that naturally. This man had not had to suffer adolescence with a birdcage strangling his teeth, or the distasteful visits to the nazi cow orthodontist either. I found myself envying him slightly.

I had just visited my dentist for my regular clean and polish. I didn't dare smile. I felt inferior. Maybe the heat was getting to me.

He pulled up a stool and stayed near me so that he could just reach under the bar without moving his great frame anytime I needed a new can. It seemed I was already his best customer, and I didn't even know his name.

"I'm Jay." I held out my hand, which was another stupid move. If this guy had a mean streak, he could crush my hand in his big paw as easily as crushing one of those small bags of potato chips you get with your burger when you don't feel like springing extra for fries.

My hand was sticking out there like a turkey drumstick in front of a kennel of starving bluetick hounds, and I couldn't very well pull it back as an afterthought. He looked me in the eye for a moment, then took my hand and shook it politely. "It's a pleasure," he said in perfect English. "I'm John. But don't you *dare* ever call me big!"

I was astounded. Since getting off the plane, I had heard a constant dialect that was completely abnormal to my ears. I kept wanting to say, "What did you just say?" but knew better than to open my mouth. Someone could be insulting my heritage, and I would blindly nod rather than draw attention to the fact that I could understand only about half the words people were speaking. I could be in northern Scotland in one of those quaint little seaside villages with all the rock huts and pick up more passing conversation.

I was surprised because before he had spoken only the confusing and unrelenting southern jargon; now he was speaking clear as a bell. "Well, John, I'm happy to meet you, and I promise...." I almost said, "I will never call you Big." I quickly recovered and finished my sentence by saying, "I'll only have one more beer."

"You ain't drivin' are you?"

"No. I just need to walk another block to my motel."

"You stayin' at the Dixy Inn?"

"Yes!" I said, sure and confident of my Internet research.

"Well, if ya havin' to stay there, don't let 'em put you in room twelve!"

"What's wrong with room twelve, John?"

"I didn't say something was wrong with it! I just said don't let 'em put you in twelve!"

I could tell I wasn't getting any more out of him on *that* subject, so I changed the channel.

"You know, John, I could give you a few tips...business tips that would greatly increase your clientele and your profitability." I was beginning to feel the generic beer. Some people say that stuff is just like water. I can attest that it is *not*. After my fourth one, I was feeling like I could be an expert on just about anything.

John feigned interest, saying, "Oh?"

"Yes! For one thing, you need a cooler...to keep the beer cold. And another you need to get a better sign. I almost missed it the window is so dirty. And if you swept up, and knocked down the cobwebs from the ceiling, and painted those atrocious water spots, you would be a lot busier. There are other things, you know...the ones I mentioned are just the basics."

"Other things?" he said, smiling enigmatically, those big, perfectly white teeth glistening.

"Well sure, John...you could *look* happier. When I first came in here, you looked downright mean. That could scare off potential customers. I know you would like to be a lot busier, so I just thought I would tip you in the right direction."

"How do you know that?"

"Well, people go into business to make money...I don't mean to be insulting, but you must be starving on the meager profits from this place."

"Do I look like I'm starving?" He stood up so I could get a good look at his physique...if you could call it that.

I shook my head. "No. I have to admit you don't, John. But what I'm talking about is getting more people through that door!"

"Don' wan' no mo' people comin' in the door!"

There was that shrill edge again. How strange, I thought. His voice was beautiful and deep...you know, the James Earl Jones type of voice, yet sometimes it seemed on the edge of cracking.

When his voice did that, it made me extremely uncomfortable.

But it was his response that stopped me in my tracks. I froze for a moment thinking of the word abstract, because for me his response was glaringly so. I've never been too good at things abstract...I'm a nuts and bolts kind of guy. Give me a wrench and a loose nut, and I'll tighten it down.

Thinking of a business that didn't want more customers really didn't compute. So my flesh and blood computer just locked right up.

John must have seen that I was about to smoke a circuit breaker, so he explained his point of view in laymen's terms.

"You see, Jay, I got my pension. Three tours in 'Nam, two purple hearts, and a disability check for some shrapnel I'm still carrying. I don't need money. I *need* peace and quiet."

He spoke the word "need" as if he were a vampire saying, I *need* blood.

"I go home, and I got a list of honey do's that never ends. Whenever I accomplish one thing on the list, the wife adds two more. Most the stuff don't need doin' anyway. Hell, if I paint the house every year like my wife wants, then my poor neighbors get to feelin' bad 'cause they home lookin' worse off'n mine. I don't want to do them poor folk that way.

"That's just an example." John started in on that perfect English again. "I love my wife—she's a sweet woman. One thing she does is listen to those evangelical radio shows all day. I can take a little of that...but *all* day?

"You see, I come here for my quiet time. I don't need any more money. If I get more customers, it won't be quiet anymore. Some of them will want a TV. I'll have to start working, which is *just* what I come here *not* to do.

"If I wash that window, more people will notice the sign. If I sweep the floor and paint, then more people will come back.

"You see those old boys playing checkers?"

I nodded my head.

"They are in the same boat as me. They are the *only* customers I need. All we want is our peace and quiet and no honey do's. You dig what I'm telling you?"

The stage curtain rose on a movie—a new movie I had never comprehended could exist. This was a private club. Somehow, I had been graced with acceptance. Honor flooded around me. I swam in bliss.

"Thanks for letting me drink here, John." Then I shut up. The silence was nice, in a strange sort of way. It was completely fresh to me.

I picked up that warm can, gulped the last swallow, and asked for another. I thought in wonderment, how much *better* the beer tasted now.

I figured I'd better not wear out my welcome. John began looking at me and then at the door. He wasn't a man of many words, and I surely didn't want him wasting some of his by asking me to leave. So after the fourth...or was it fifth beer, I nodded quietly, thanking him again in silence, grabbed my bags, and headed for the door.

Just as I opened it, and the afternoon heat hit me in the face like a brick, he said, "Don' go forgettin' what I tol' you about room twelve!"

I nodded again and departed.

Chapter 3

Fortunately, I was on the home stretch. The motel was less than a block away. I began thinking desperately about the pool and wondering how long it would take me to strip out of my steaming, soggy clothes, and don my swimming trunks.

The sign loomed ahead. I say loomed because it had some green crud growing on it, and the little voice that sometimes speaks in my head said, "It wasn't like that in the Internet photos of the place." A sense of foreboding came over me, and I started wondering what the pool would look like.

The office was cool. That was promising, I thought, as the woman rasped something about pets and I assured her I would be the only living thing staying in the room. At least I *think* it was a woman talking to me. She looked a lot like Jackie Gleason. I began checking my memory bank for obituaries. Could Gleason still be alive? I found myself wondering. Could he have run from the spotlight, bought a rinky-dink motel in a has-been town in northern Alabama, and escaped into oblivion?

When she handed me the key, I almost fainted. It could have been the heat, but I think there was more. I could see John's big white teeth when he gave me the advice about *not* taking room number twelve.

"Don't you have any other rooms," I asked, my heart palpitating. "I have a thing about the number twelve...you see...." I was about to make up some outlandish reason for my aversion when she cut me off, saying there was a contractor's crew in town, and that she had held the room for me...in good faith, even though the *contractor* had offered to pay more than the going rate.

Then she glared. Silence set in.

I stumbled a bit verbally, and she, coiled and ready to strike at any sign of weakness, spouted, "Are you one of those superstitious types?!"

I immediately thought of voodoo and witchcraft and how there were twelve apostles, and what she might think, and how that stuff would be viewed down here. I recovered with strength and gracefulness.

I mumbled, "Okay," took the key, and thought about leaving with my tail between my legs.

She had won the first round. I had the sneaking suspicion there would be more rounds to come.

She pointed, without speaking, and I took that to mean I was free to go. I went, but not without thinking of how these southern people could take silence to a *whole* new realm.

I opened the door to room twelve and got the usual second-class motel odors—must, Lysol, and rug deodorant.

The air conditioner was one of those after-thoughts stuck in the hole of an empty window. It was throbbing and sputtering sickly. I reached over and felt the air coming out of it. It felt about as cool as the second beer I'd had at John's place. Anyway, the room was better than outside, so I closed the door.

I was about to throw my bag on the bed when I noticed something that had completely slipped quietly into the back of the old data bank. There was that gooey spot that was brownish green on the side of my biggest bag. It had dried in the heat and looked like it would start crumbling, flaking, and falling onto the floor any second. I still didn't care to believe it was what it looked like, so I made way with haste into the bathroom and opened the shower door.

The shower appeared to be clean...that was encouraging at least. I turned the water on and held the bag up close so the spray could do the work. I had nothing to scrub with, at least nothing I wanted to come in contact with whatever the spot was. As soon as the hot water hit the mess, all doubt was removed.

When I had thrown my bag in the back of that man's pick-up truck, it had landed smack-dab in the middle of you know what! Yuck! Nasty...yuk! I hadn't been in Alabama ten minutes, and I had landed in it!

I just hoped fervently that this wasn't some kind of omen. If it was, it couldn't possibly be good. I thought about what the person at the front desk had asked about being superstitious, and I laughed to myself. You know, like a grown man does when he hears some freaky sound in the pitch black of night. You laugh just to make yourself comfortable, and because grown men aren't supposed to be afraid of the dark. There is nothing funny about being spooked in the darkness. So why was I laughing? I asked myself, trembling slightly.

I tried to turn off the rumbling train of my thoughts, but they kept coming, racing down the track, going back to those big white teeth saying, "Not room twelve!"

I peeled off my clothes after getting the bag kind of back to normal and donned the vacation trunks. These babies had been my good-luck piece. I had bought them just before going on my first book tour. They had seen me through a ton of cities and some very interesting circumstances. If only they could talk, I thought, as I left my room and went in search of the pool.

I was devastated. You know how pools are supposed to have that inviting crystal blue water? I mean, you know that there will be the inevitable and overpowering stench of chlorine when you jump in, but that's just to protect you from those billions of nasty germs and bacteria that love festering in eighty degree plus water when droves of people climb in and some of them, especially children, do the unspeakable.

Well, what greeted me was green. It wasn't even a pretty green—you know, like the kind you see around St. Patrick's Day…cheerful…happy. No, this green looked like it might be hiding the creature from the black lagoon beneath its sinister surface.

I stormed back to the office, my body temperature reaching dangerously close to the redline zone. I opened the door and walked into the inviting cool. It did nothing to change my mood. Noticing a great big spanking new, shiny, industrial air conditioning unit on the office wall didn't calm me either.

Jackie Gleason's double was still behind the counter. I stammered in disbelief, "The pool!"

"Pool's broken."

Pool's broken, she says, as if I hadn't figured that one out. "Well, call the pool man. I rented a room with a pool!"

"Pool man dead," she said, without looking up from her *National Enquirer*.

"What?!"

"Got shot a few weeks back. Drug deal or sump'in'. No pool man, no pool."

"Well then…call someone else!"

"I did, but since the pool man was shot here, in *this* establishment...respectable people been keepin' their distance."

Not only was there no pool, and no pool man, but now she was insinuating that I was not a respectable personage. "See here now!" I said with authority, "you can't advertise a pool and not have one that is in working order!"

Ralph Nader will have a field day with this! I thought, still fuming.

"Ad don't say the pool works, just says it's heated. Sun's heatin' it right now. The water ain't cold. Go ahead and jump in if you're overheated. It won't kill you."

"You're kidding, right?!"

She didn't say anything, just turned a page on her rag sheet, like it was more important than our conversation.... There was that damn...frustrating southern silence again.

I began, "Well I have a mind to...!"

She cut me off mid-sentence and said, "If you don't like the pool, I suggest you better take a *real* cold shower!

"Now are you goin' ta leave me be an quit your *pestering*? Or do I call the chief!"

"The chief?" I asked, while thinking that she had just relegated me to the myriads of creepy crawly pests that you exterminate with a spray can.

"The cops...! You know, the men in blue suits! 'Cause I'm feelin' threatened here! You don' wan' me tellin' them you been threatenin' me, do ya?"

She was serious.... I had made the decision that *it* was a she that I was speaking to, because below the whiskers I saw unsavory jiggles when she lifted her chin to talk. Try as I did, I could not keep my eyes from wandering down there into no man's land just to prove to my unbelieving brain that this was *not* a man.

She raised her eyebrows threateningly. That was enough...I'd had it! I turned around and marched back to my room like any honorable soldier would do when retreating from sure and instantaneous death.

I didn't even take my shorts off. I just climbed into the shower and turned the cold water on full. She had been right. It did cool me down.

After my shower, I pulled the coverlet on the bed back. Any dunce knows that while a motel like this *should* change and wash the sheets every day, the bedspread was fair game to go months without tending.

Now a myriad of unspeakable things can happen on a made bed. Some of them very pleasantly exciting, yet I had no intention of mixing my bodily essence with the history of infamous room twelve. I lay back, relaxing; my heart had stopped racing.

I was just getting comfortable when I felt an itch beginning on my legs below the knees. I didn't think much of it. I just involuntarily scratched it like any relaxed person will do.

Then it spread to my thighs.

Something was wrong! I thought frantically. I jumped up from the bed just as I felt the itch beginning on my chest. I was scratching all over now, as I attempted in vain to keep ahead of the spread.

Then it dawned on me. I had used the motel soap! In the heat of my fixation about the pool, or lack of a usable pool, I had forgotten to use my hypo-allergenic soap.

I jumped to my bag, which was drying nicely, and tore at the zipper like a man goes for his fly after drinking way too much coffee before being trapped on a very slow bus. This time, however, I was not fighting time to keep my bladder from exploding. I was racing the clock to save myself from giant moving hives.

If you've ever had a hive, I pity you. If you have ever had moving hives, we are bonded by insufferable misery. If you have ever experienced giant moving hives, I congratulate you for still being amongst the living. It would be easier just to hold a gun to your head for a last painful second before pulling the trigger and ending the torment. That is if you had a gun, and if you could stop itching for that second before you, with valor and insanity shining in your eyes, pulled the trigger.

I ripped open my bag, not caring if I tore it to shreds. I pawed with frenzy! Carefully packed belongings were flying like chips from a wood shredder around the room. I needed my bathroom kit!

Eureka! I felt like a prospector, who after grueling years of searching and digging, has finally come to the mother lode.

I sprinted the two steps to the bathroom. I leapt into the shower.

Fortunately, I had caught it in time. I had nipped the evil cheap chain motel soap where it hurts. I had saved myself. At last…I could rest.

The bed was a heaven of sorts after my trying day. I hadn't eaten anything since the wonder-food aboard the plane, and I didn't care. I was determined to sleep and worry about foraging for nutrition later.

The mattress was comfortable. I lay there over-thinking and comparing all the motel mattresses I had slept on in the past year. Well, not all of them. Mostly I remember the worst and the best, the in-betweens get lost in that unmemorable foggy area. This one was not exceptional. Tonight I would rate it between a six and a seven as motel mattresses go…except for one spot.

It was kind of a lump...but not quite. There seemed to be an indentation as well. The bump had a pocket in the middle. The pocket was much like one of those juicy and painful adolescent pimples you have popped, hoping the crater that is left in the explosive wake will heal before you begin serious dating.

Yes, there was definitely something odd there.

I got up wearily. I knew I could not sleep until I had solved the mystery of the pocketed bump. Stripping the bedding back from the headboard down to what would be chest level, I saw the bump clearly beneath the absorbent mattress cover.

Now my curiosity was piqued. I hastily ripped back the cover and gasped.

There was a big dark spot...and a hole about the size of my little finger. It couldn't be! Or could it?! I thought frantically.

Then I heard Big...no not Big. Never call him Big! My mind ran in circles...John's deep voice flooded my consciousness: "Remember what I tol' ya about room twelve."

I packed the shambles of my strewn clothing into my bag, grabbed my lifesaving hypoallergenic soap and bath kit, shouldered one bag, and rolled the other right past the female Jackie Gleason and towards Big...no, not Big!...to John's place. All during this, I was thinking about one mattress I would *never* forget—the one with the bullet hole.

He was the only friend I had in this town. Maybe he knew a good place where I could rest from the traumatized state into which I had been recently molded.

Fortunately, there were lights on at John's establishment. It was about the dinner hour, so I was happily relieved when I opened the door and found his great, reassuring bulk sitting behind the makeshift pallets and plywood.

The look on my face brought concern out on his own. I must have looked like a gunshot victim myself because I felt nearly as injured after my encounter with the horrors of the Dixy Inn.

"You all right, man?" he asked, sincerity and compassion ringing in that big...I mean deep voice of his.

"Yeah...yeah, I'm alright. The room...they only had twelve...I had no choice."

"Didn't I tell you not to take that room?!!"

"Yes...you did. I was tired...the beer...the trip...the heat...that thing...I mean the woman at the desk...!"

"You mean Jackie Gleason?"

"Gleason's dead. Been dead for decades...can't be him. He never was anything like Elvis!"

"Calm down, man!" John reached under the bar and pulled out my salvation from within its dark confines. He popped the top for me. I tipped the can upside down and when there was nothing left in it, I began sucking on it like a baby will when his bottle is empty.

John pulled another can, handed it to me, and I felt its reassuring weight in my hand. Then I opened it, and settled down.

"In the future, when Big John gives you advice...you gonna listen?"

I shook my head up and down without taking my lips from that second can. When I stopped, I said, "You told me never to call you Big John. But you do?"

Those beautiful white teeth appeared and he said, "Only *my* friends call me Big...I guess it'd be all right if you...did sometimes, too. But only when we're alone. I spent a lot a time breakin' people of that tendency. I don't want you starting people thinking they can get away with it, too!"

I smiled back at him. He was the *only* friend I had in town. I liked the way he had said "Breakin'." It had a *really* nice ring.

We sat in silence with only an occasional train rolling by "breakin'" it. Finally, he said, "I know a place that would be good for you. But you have to promise me you won't drink alcohol there. Mimi don't tolerate drinking at her establishment."

I nodded assent and said, "Mimi?"

"Yeah. Come on. I was just about to lock up when you came dragging in here. I sure am glad I didn't. The sidewalks are about to roll *right* up! You'd a had to go on back to Jackie."

John started laughing, and it was a sound that I found wondrous. It started out like distant thunder, then broke into a bass chorus that made me think of the old spiritual, "Swing Low, Sweet Chariot." His laugh was a gift from heaven, and when it came, it was rumbling out of *my* new friend.

When I reminded him that I owed him twelve bits for the two beers, he laughed some more and even harder, as if I had struck his funny bone by chance.

He replied, "Not tonight! Your show has been worth a *lot* more than that!" Then that gorgeous rumble began all over again. It didn't stop, and I began laughing, too, right along with him.

Chapter 4

I SPENT THE first few days staying at Mimi's, acclimatizing to the heat. I was also attempting to learn enough to understand the local dialect while being force-fed by a loving, black, butterball of a woman whose children had all moved away from Mussel Shoals. I felt adopted. It was like being back in my sweet, nurturing grandmother's house. Savory scents wafted out of the kitchen all hours of the day.

It was wonderful, for the first few hours.

I liked Mimi a lot. I also needed a beer and some uninterrupted quiet time where I could think without unending interruptions. Since I couldn't drink in her house, even secretly because I had promised Big John, I needed to get out regularly. This brought me daily to his private club. Everything was fine...except I wasn't writing a word. Well, I had written a word or two, but so far they were forced words.

If you've ever attempted to take writing seriously, you have probably searched out the writer's Holy Grail. No? Well I have. It consists of the co-mingled pool of classic and modern works of the masters and their philosophies of writing style.

Now, writers are a secretive and protective lot. I mean, if you ever reach that far-flung star of limited success and can actually live on the scraps you earn writing...would you really share with others who are competing for the sparkling crowns in the industry by giving away your trade secrets? Of course not! I just answered that quandary for those of you who thought most writers would.

I am different though. Or so different my ex-wife divorced me saying I was childish. I thanked her for the compliment, packed my belongings, and happily left the person who had spent the better part of my so-called adult life trying to make me grow up. I didn't want to. I still don't.

My favorite passage in the New Testament is where Christ tells his twelve Apostles, "Lest ye be like little children, you cannot enter the Kingdom of God." Amen to that, brother!

Anyway, back to the Holy Grail, or my meager interpretation of it.

You see, some authors write a minimum of words per day. Jack London's goal was a thousand. Now he wasn't fortunate enough to have a modern day laptop, so running to the store constantly for bottles of Wite-Out to fix his typos probably slowed his productivity down a bit.

Please keep in mind that when I was young and discovered *The Call of The Wild*, I began the London adventure. My eyes were opened to a wondrous new world of competition, suffering, victory, despair, death, and effervescent joy—among many other things. His talented fingers, driven by his curiosity and creative mind, could take my imagination on a whirlwind tour any time I parted the cover of one of his many treasured works.

Also keep in mind that Jack died in his mid-thirties, a hopeless alcoholic—a truly sad ending to a life unparalleled. Maybe that goal of so many words a day created too much pressure...who knows. I don't abide by the so many words a day theory.

Other masters would tell you that inspiration is the key, that if you open your mind to the cosmos, or God, or the infinite intelligence of the universe, that ideas and words will flow into you like an intravenous drip.

The problem is that you could spend a hell of a lot of time waiting for those pearls of inspiration and never get a word down on paper.

Then there are the architects of writing; they can conjugate a verb, dangle a participle properly, and construct sentences that take an expert in literary archeology to unearth and make modern sense of.

To be honest, when it comes to describing a verb, a pronoun, an adjective, or any of those structured sides of literacy, I flee in embarrassment. I have a certain dyslexia when it comes to dissecting a sentence and labeling all the parts like it was a frog on the table in seventh grade biology. Where is the romance in that?

God created editors for us writers. Now we are free. I want to feel the wind in my hair, like I was that young boy just learning to ride a bicycle.

Remember when you learned to ride a bike? Sure, you suffered a few scrapes and bruises from falling, but you were brave. You picked yourself up and, after a bit of struggling, you were set free. Writing should be like that. Feel the wind in your hair and explore those unknown streets.

Now, back to my theory...or maybe blueprint would be a better word.

I have forced words onto the page and then realized there was no point in the exercise...if the product stinks. Why do that to myself? I could be at the beach, enjoying the sun and a parade of interesting people, getting a bit of color onto the pages of my pale complexion rather than sweating before a laptop, hoping by the end of my frustrating session that I could salvage a gram of wit or intrinsic value from the tasteless, mundane black and white I had just painfully created, an embarrassment...most of the time.

Some would say you *can* go back through that trash, doctor it up, healing the broken wings of literary flight. I say why bother? It is more trouble to fix a crappy set of forced writing than it is to sit down and write something your heart tells you to.

Inspirational writing is a gift from the great unknown, and any aspiring writer has surely glimpsed its power and bounty. But waiting can be hell. I mean waiting for those raindrops.

I realized was writing a diatribe on writing. I was not writing the story I had traveled nearly three thousand miles to capture.

I decided I had better get out of the house and take a drive.

Chapter 5

I HAD RENTED a car so that I wasn't forced to walk everywhere in the grueling heat and humidity anymore. The thing even had an air conditioner that worked. Blessed cool, I thought happily. I would drive just so I could get away from the heat, and so that I could see the countryside. There was a lot of countryside to see, and most of it looked pretty much the same.

I did find one area I liked in particular and drove there just to see if there might be a little house for rent. The road wound along a river channel that grew giant trees along both sides. The shade was heavenly, there were fields and small farms, and the places were well kept.

I was just tooling along enjoying the day when about a quarter mile ahead I saw a woman walking alongside the road. My attention was focused immediately on her... I mean on the way she walked. She had a rhythm to her steps that was gracefully smooth.

The woman was wearing a conservative white dress with some kind of floral pattern. It was not revealing. It fell just below her knees. There was some lace that swished back and forth along the hem, but my eyes were above that.

What I noticed first was the way her stride worked that...those muscles in her upper...I mean there are a lot of words in the English language that people use to name a woman's...but none of them seemed to match what I was so wrapped up in watching.

I stepped on the brake lightly and slowed down, so I would not pass the entrancing sight too quickly.

I went to a hypnotist once in my twenties because I had desperately wanted to quit smoking. Believe it or not, the treatment worked. Watching this woman walk along, I was reminded of how I'd felt back then. I was powerless to quit staring at the gentle swish back and forth of...her... loveliness. It caught and held my attention. I could feel my eyes first moving side to side, so as not to miss a bit of the movement. It was like the Edgar Allan Poe story, "The Pit and the Pendulum." I was transfixed on the swing. Before another moment passed, my entire head was sweeping gently side to side in time with the motion.

I slowed down some more.

It wasn't just the way it swung; it was way more than that. It was the shape, the size, and the fluidity that had me entranced. I was wondering what her face looked like as I neared her, and at that moment, as if in answer to my questioning mind, she turned and looked right through me. I felt like I was in the spirit world and she were my guardian angel...a heavenly being...ethereal, mesmerizing, engulfing. I pressed the brake down involuntarily. With that look, she had captured me.

A light smile graced her tanned face, a slim upward curving line of white teeth shone. Her hair was dark and wavy, full of body, and her eyes...those vast, dark brown eyes...they looked right into mine.

I rolled down the passenger window and asked, "Can I give you a lift? It's pretty hot out to be walking this afternoon, Miss."

I was hoping two things desperately: That she *was* a Miss, and that she would accept my offer.

She glanced down the road, and her profile struck my heart like a knife. Her nose was neither large nor too small. It had a slight aristocratic rise on the bridge. The rise was barely noticeable. She looked back and asked in normal English, "Are you from around here?"

I knew if I said no, I was finished.

I responded not by lying but by stretching the truth a little. "I'm an old friend of Big John's. I'm here for the summer writing a piece about Mussel Shoals."

First off, "old" was a relative term...I was getting older by the minute, and how "old" did a friendship have to be, to be considered old? I have had some friendships that got *very* old rather quickly, so I figured I was on stable ground.

"Who would want to read about Mussel Shoals?"

She had me there. So I improvised. "A lot of people, I hope. There wouldn't be much sense in me spending the *entire* summer down here if there weren't plenty of folks interested in Mussel Shoals and its history." I had emphasized the word entire so she would understand I wasn't some tourist.

She looked at me kind of funny and said, "History." It wasn't a question, or a statement, so I let it go.

"You would honor me, and make the day worthwhile, if I could drive you to where you're going." That was pretty smooth, I thought, complimentary and not too desperate. I gave her my warmest smile and showed some teeth...but not too many. I didn't want to look like a wolf.

"It is pretty hot out here, and it just wouldn't do to perspire through my dress, now would it?"

I agreed immediately, put the car in park, jumped out, skipped lightly around the front end of it, and opened the door for her.

"Are all Yankee boys as polite as you?" she said, smiling and looking me straight in the eyes once more.

"Well, ma'am, my mother raised me to treat women this way...."

"Bless her heart."

"I'm Jay...Jay VanVessey. Will you grace me with your name?"

"Leilauna. You can call me Lei, if you'd like something shorter."

"Leilauna...I like that. I think the longer version suits you...Leilauna," I repeated, and she smiled at me again, only this time it was the real deal. She had cute little dimples when she smiled wide. I helped her in and closed the door.

Whoee! I thought. The day had just improved immensely.

She had no wedding ring on, and I knew any young lady down here in the Deep South who had a regular suitor would not ride with a stranger. Well I *had* used Big John as a reference.

As if she had picked up on my thoughts, she asked, "How long have you known John?"

Uh-oh.... "Well...it seems like we met just last week... but when I look back on all the things we've been through together, it seems like a lifetime, too."

Whew! That was close. I reminded myself not to stretch the truth in this small town anymore. I also reminded myself to talk with Big John and see if he would be gracious enough to corroborate my explanation.

I got the car moving, even if it were very slowly. I think she noticed because she kept looking over at me and then at the speedometer. When she did that, her gorgeous smile would pop out again.

I found myself driving slower and slower until we were barely moving.

I don't think I've ever enjoyed a movie as much as I did that little video in my mind...of her framed in the side window, greens, browns, and colors of straw passed behind her in a moving collage of living color, and she was there in the middle of it, turning and flashing smiles at me.

The car stopped. She looked at me kind of funny and said, "Don't you think we should get moving?"

I snapped out of my trance, laughed, and said lightly, "I was just wanting this drive to last forever. There is something *very* special about you."

"I'm glad you noticed. It's nice what you said…about the ride lasting forever."

"Yes…" I stumbled over the words in anticipation. "Could we…could we go out sometime?" I asked lamely.

"Oh!" She was actually stunned. She started in a pleasantly dismissive manner, "I couldn't possibly…I mean you seem very nice and everything, but…."

"It's okay, I know I'm quite a bit older than you."

"Jay, it isn't your age…it's about what people would think. This is a small town, and…oh! You can drop me right up here!"

She was pointing towards a white building. It was kind of different looking. Then, as we drove out from under a tree, I saw the steeple."

I turned reluctantly into the parking area. I could feel the rain clouds moving in. The hopes I had felt so wonderfully a few moments ago shriveled.

She smiled quickly and said most politely, "You see, I teach the young children Sunday school here. I'm not interested in dating men. I feel married to Christ."

"I'm happy for you," I lied. Well, what was I supposed to say? My brain was recovering from shock. There we were, destined to be new and possibly intimate friends, and she lets me know I'll always be second best, or worse.

"I have to go. I enjoyed talking with you. If you happen to be up this way…I thought the ride was nice, too."

She throws me a shred of desperate hope and I cling to it, like a piece of fractured timber when my ship is wrecked and I'm floating out, far from land.

"What days do you walk here?" I asked, my outlook brightening.

"Most afternoons. I like the exercise, and I get the church all to myself. I can make lesson plans for the little ones and worship."

I jumped right into the swing of things. "Jesus said, 'Whenever two or more are gathered in my name they are my church.' I could come in with you. Then there *would* be two people."

"Jesus is always with me…so I'm never alone. There are always two of us. Good day, Mr. VanVessey."

I drove away thinking that my knowledge of the Bible hadn't softened her a bit. Then I thought of never being alone with her, and of having to share her with *Him*.

I can't remember thinking about anything in particular as I drove, everything was just a bit blurred—a thick mist rolled through my mind, befuddling rational thought. There was spinning, and I realized I had better stop the car because I was feeling quite odd.

Parking along the side of the road, I jumped out of the car. I was short of breath, my heart was pounding, and I suddenly realized that everything I was feeling, the daze I was in and the dizziness, was because of her.

My thinking cleared a bit, and I got back in the car. I headed straight for Big John's, praying all the way that he would be there.

Chapter 6

ONE OF THE best things about Mussel Shoals is the downtown parking. There is tons of it. I drove up right in front of John's and didn't have to parallel park. I just slid up to the curb at about thirty, slammed on the brakes, jumped out of the car, and rushed in.

"What in the hell are you doin', boy?" John exclaimed in a booming voice.

I looked around and the place was empty, as usual. *Good!* I thought. I was going to spill my guts. I needed some serious advice, some information, and an understanding ear. I needed a beer.

"Boy, I can see you got your tail in a knot! What are you up to?" he asked. His curiosity was killing him.

"It's a woman, John! She's the most gorgeously beautiful creature I've ever seen!"

"Shit man! How old *are* you?"

I couldn't answer. I had grabbed a beer, popped the top, and slipped it to my lips in one fluid motion. I was in the middle of something important and couldn't be disturbed. His question was rhetorical anyway.

"For your information, gorgeously beautiful is redundant. I thought you were a writer?"

"With her," I began, after setting the beer down and taking a deep breath, "the redundancy does not become a negative to the art of her description. It merely magnifies the picture and makes it more powerful." I was on a roll, boasting loudly on the shriveled hope that I might possibly have a chance.

"Man, you going to start spouting Shakespeare? I hope not. Will you tell me who she is?"

"Leilauna," I whimpered.

"Shit man, are you crazy comin' in here like this? This ain't New York City! You dig me? This be Baptist country. Her church requires chaperoned dates. They do not dance, nor do they drink."

He looked at the foam on my upper lip. "And they sure as hell don't like Yankees comin' down here and starting something with the Sunday school teacher. Are you crazy?"

"You asked me that twice."

"Yeah! And I'll keep asking! Not to mention she's in her early twenties, and how old are you Jay?"

I tried to look sheepish, but it was no use. He saw right through it.

"Just break it to me, John, do I have a chance?"

"You got a snow-ball's chance in the fires of hell," he said. "That's what you got. Just give it up, man. Come back to reality.

"How old are you?" he asked again. Only this time, there was no ignoring it. That strange shrill edge had come back into his voice. I hadn't heard it since my first day in Mussel Shoals.

"Thirty-seven."

"Don't shit me, man," he said. "You gonna start lyin' to Big John?" The shrill edge came again. I was on dangerous ground. I could see my membership card to his club going up in smoke. I leveled.

"Forty-six."

"Damn straight! Thirty-seven. Who you think I am, man? Some watermelon that just fell off the truck? Don't you ever be tellin' me no lie. I'll kick your ass! And then I'll boot it right out of here. You understan' me?"

"Yes."

I felt like I was fourteen again, standing in front of my mother at four in the morning when she had caught me slipping back in my bedroom window. She had been waiting in my room. I wasn't any smoother today than I was then, I thought.

"All right," he said, "enough of the wounded little boy look. I ain't falling for that shit either.... She *is* really something though, isn't she?"

I looked up, completely surprised. He was smiling, and that big rumbling laugh set in. We both laughed for a long time at what a complete idiot I had instantly become.

Chapter 7

THE NEXT AFTERNOON, I was out the door from Mimi's and walking to my rental car when I noticed I was whistling. I never whistle. Never say never, I guess.

I jumped in and drove to the river road hoping desperately that I would see her.

I could have driven up the river straight from town, but I didn't for two reasons. I took a circuitous back route so that I would be going the same direction as the day before. When and if I were fortunate enough to see her again, I wanted to drive up behind her...so that...I could revere once more the heavenly...stride she possessed.

Coming around a shaded corner, I saw a small lavender dot in the distance. As I came nearer, I was certain it was her. I would recognize her walk amongst a throng. We were much farther from the church than the day before. She must live quite a ways up the river, I thought.

I let off the gas and slowed down. I wanted to savor the moment. Before long, as my car slid quietly up from the rear like a prowling and hungry tiger shark, she turned. Seeing me, she broke into that enchanting smile once more. It was a smile that had kept me awake most of the previous night.

She appeared before me like a dream. I knew today that the vision would last longer than it had the day before. We were nearly four miles from the church.

I didn't ask this time. I just rolled down the window and greeted her as I stopped. Then I jumped out quickly before she had time to object and, skating around the car, opened her door with a subtle flourish. *Her door,* I thought...I only prayed it would become hers.

"You are too kind!" She touched me lightly on the forearm and my whole body set to tingling immediately. She had electricity. It was like she was a cell phone tower, and I was her biggest minute user.

I trotted in athletic gracefulness the seven paces back to my door, climbed in, and started the car into a rolling crawl. Leilauna was mine for the drive. I planned to milk it for as long as she would allow me to.

I didn't say a word. I just stared into those eyes. I was happy with that. My brain was numb. I didn't know if I could speak without uttering gibberish, so I played it safe. I was the mysterious quiet one.

She broke the unhealthy silence. "Mr. VanVessey...."

I jumped right into the conversation before it was my turn. "Please, call me Jay. My father was called Mr. VanVessey."

"Is he no longer with us, Jay?"

Oh, how she spoke my name! I had never thought of my name as being special until it rolled off her lips so pleasantly. "No. My parents both passed some years ago. It was difficult...I'm just now getting over it." *Sympathy...let her know you need kindness and compassionate sympathy,* I thought.

"Oh! You poor dear!"

She reached over and placed her hand on mine. I had purposely left it dangling a little on her side of the center console, so she didn't have to reach very far. Then as quickly as it came, she removed hers.

"How far do you live up the road, Leilauna?"

"A few more miles."

"You mean you walk seven miles to church, and then seven miles back home?"

"Yes, but it doesn't take me long. I walk very fast."

"I noticed that," I said, attempting to keep the conversation moving. "You know, Leilauna, that's about fourteen miles. It must take you a couple of hours each way."

"I do it in an hour and a half. I'm in *really* great shape—my legs are like iron."

"Yes, I can imagine that...they are."

Was it just me? Was I reading something into the conversation that she did not intend? *Shut up, Jay!* I thought.

"If I picked you up farther up the road, we could spend more time talking, and get you to church much quicker."

"Jay, I couldn't possibly impose on you like that!"

"I could drive you back, too."

"You are such a sweetheart. What would you want in return for that? So much of your time, I mean, and your gas. Gas is so expensive these days."

There it was again, the tidbit dangled. Was I imagining things?

"I assure you I have been bored out of my mind. I would love nothing more than to be your own personal chauffeur. Besides, I'm new around here. I've been hoping to meet a friend."

"What would people think, Jay? When they see us together all the time?" She went on. "Gossip runs rampant here. I couldn't stand being the topic. I hope you understand."

I was dashed, my dream shattered before my very eyes. I drove on in silence.

"I guess you *could* pick me up a little closer to my farm. I did kind of twist my ankle in the barn this morning. I was going out to milk the cow and stepped on a rotten board.

My foot went through the floor, and my ankle bent wrong. That old place needs some work."

I stopped the car. "My father was a doctor. He taught me lots of things, especially about ankles, and about carpentry, and handy-man stuff. That was his hobby. Can I take a look?"

"If you think you could do me some good…I mean, if you keep your hands below the knee, I guess there would be no sin."

She lifted her leg and above her ankle, I could see a bruise. It was small, and there was no apparent swelling, but I didn't tell her that.

"Oh yes, that definitely needs some attention."

"What kind of attention, doctor?"

"I should rub it. You see an injury like that needs the circulation stimulated. That will make the swelling and the bruised feeling go away faster."

"If you say so."

I took her ankle and gently rubbed it. I was in heaven. I was imagining her rising early in the morning, with me, coffee in hand, watching her walk out to milk the cow. I started moving my hand up her lower calf, explaining that the ankle muscles ran up into it. She allowed me to, and while I rubbed, I heard the softest little moan from deep in her throat.

"Am I hurting you?" I asked.

"No, it feels real nice."

Her eyes had been closed, and they suddenly shot open. She pulled her leg back quickly and said, "Car coming, let's go!"

My bubble burst. I followed orders, cursing the damn farmer who had the audacity to use this road—*our* road.

The rest of the trip was pretty uneventful. I hoped I hadn't offended her because she didn't say much, and she smiled very subtly. I made small talk and let her know I was from Seattle.

She commented that she had always wanted to visit there, and I offered to host her. She looked at me silently for a few moments and then said, "I just don't think I could leave the children. No, that would be wrong. My *duty* is here."

We were at the church. I was disappointed. The time had streaked by even though I had done less than ten miles per hour. She thanked me politely for the ride and stepped out.

Just as she closed the door, she said, through the dwindling opening, "I'll be walking back around seven. It will be getting pretty dark by then."

I nodded in rapt disbelief. I had her return schedule locked into the vault of my intellect. I was a happy man.

Chapter 8

At seven fifteen, I was driving the river road. I had been back to Mimi's. She had served pot roast and various other melt in your mouth treasures that made my eyes bulge and tugged at my greedy stomach.

I had eaten enough to barely satisfy Mimi. She kept pushing food towards me. I refused for the last time, and I saw a determined look pop up on her well-rounded face. She looked like she was considering wrestling me down and force-feeding me. I got a bit worried because she would have a distinct advantage in a wrestling match. She outweighed me a hundred pounds plus.

I complimented her culinary efforts and offered to assist clearing the table. I really didn't want to do all that. I was just trying to bring closure to something that should last less time than the New York City Marathon. I started understanding why there are so many obese people; they all probably had mothers like Mimi.

"You would just slow me down. I have my system, and I can tell you have plans this evening. Who are you seeing?" she asked.

Now *that* was a fairly innocent question, but when you looked at Mimi's expression, you knew differently. She was diving right in.

"No one, Mimi. I was thinking about going for a drive, maybe to the next town, you know, see the sights."

Ain't nothing worth seein' over there, that you can't see right here in Mussel Shoals."

"Well, just the same. Thank you again for dinner."

All I wanted to do was take a shower, shave, and decide what clothes I should wear. She looked at me with knowing eyes. She was searching for info. She could have hung me upside down and water boarded me. I would have taken it for hours without giving her a shred. My life was a private thing. Well, private between me and Big John.

Still, was I that obvious? I thanked her and went on my way.

I had expected to see Leilauna much closer to the church.

I was five miles past the church where the road began heading slightly uphill, out of the flat farm country and breaking into elevated forest land, co-mingled with bits and pieces of pasture. It was near dark, but not enough to need headlights. Coming around a corner, I saw lavender and it was moving very...pleasantly.

I reined up my mount beside her and was out the door and around the car in a flash. "Good evening, Leilauna," I said, opening *her* car door. "I was worried I had missed you. How's the ankle?"

She made a move to get in and stopped, gazing at me with a puzzled look, like maybe it was appraisal. "Much better! Thanks, Jay," she said, then she got in.

YeeeHaaa! I thought. She obviously trusted me. *For once in my life,* I thought, *a woman with impeccable and discerning taste.*

"Just let me know where to turn," I said, as the car began moving.

"I will."

It was a pleasant silence—I mean the lack of words between us. After a bit she said, "Take a right, at that mailbox."

I turned in, and there was only a gravel road with nothing but trees growing up to its edge. Some of them were immense. We kept going slightly uphill, and before long, the trees opened into pasture and then an idyllic farm setting: Hand-hewn cabin and barn, and an old Volkswagen Beetle, which ironically had been my first car. I had wrenched my way through high school putting that old bug back into mint condition. When it wasn't cool anymore, it had been sold.

"Who's car?"

"It was my grandmother's. It's mine now, but it doesn't run. I inherited this place from her. I've been working on it a little...the farm...I'm embarrassed to say, is pretty run down."

"As I said, I'm really handy at fix and repair stuff. And your car, well I bet I could get that running in a jiffy!"

"Oh, I couldn't possibly...you've already done so much... my ankle...and these very nice rides...thank you. I better go!"

"Leilauna, it's dark. Let me at least walk you up to the front door. Is your porch light burned out?"

"This is unheard of where *you* come from but...I don't have a porch light. I don't have electricity...I have some lanterns. My Gram had a generator and batteries that store the electricity, but I don't know anything about those things. I'm afraid to use that old generator. It looks like Gram bought it when she was still young."

She laughed a little, but this was not the laugh of someone having fun. She was obviously embarrassed. I had seen a slight flush beneath her tanned skin.

"Really, Leilauna, I would be happy to do some work around here for you. You don't have to pay me."

"I really couldn't...take your help. It wouldn't seem right."

"Hey! I've got a great idea. I want to move from Mimi's. John recommended me there, and it's been great and all, but I would really like to rent a small house for the summer. You know a lot of people in your church. Maybe one of them has a vacant place they would like to rent out for the summer. I don't need much.

"Then, you've helped me! See? Then it would be completely natural for me to give you a hand around here. I could help you. Call it a finder's fee on setting me up in a good little quiet spot where I can write in peace."

"Well, it seems kind of strange.... Do you have the necessary tools?" she asked, obviously tempted.

"Tools...no! That's no problem! I can pick the few things I need up second hand, and John has all the tools. He always talks about his home improvement projects."

"I'll think about what you said. I don't want you asking to borrow John's tools... If I accept your offer. I wouldn't want you telling people you were my handy-man...even if you were...I just don't see it. This is such a small town, what would people think? If it got around I mean?"

I was willing to swear most anything for the opportunity to help around Leilauna's. I didn't really know as much about doctoring as I had said. I knew a lot less about carpentry and handy-man work, but how hard could it be? I mean everyone knows that's the kind of work in which the uneducated partake. Besides, I remember seeing a big building supply company offering how-to books on just about anything.

"You have nothing to worry about. I will be the image and definition of discretion," I said. "I will be the ninja handy-man! You know how those guys operate—no one ever sees them, but the dirty work gets done!"

She got out of the car without giving me an answer. I jumped out, intending to walk with her to the door.

"Jay, I'll be fine on my own. Please don't walk me up."

Her face had a look I'd never seen before. It spoke of her humble, run-down inherited farm and how she would love some help with it, but the local religious crowd would not approve if they knew.

I wanted to kiss her right there. She looked so vulnerable. The rescuer inside of me was polishing his armor and saddling the trusty stead. I would be back…with tools! I thought all this loudly in my brain, while out loud I said, softly, "Goodnight, Leilauna."

"Goodnight, Jay. Thanks for the ride. Oh! I hate…I've been putting off asking…but you don't drink, do you?"

"Alcohol…? No…! Never touch the stuff…Hate it!"

"That's good. My church doesn't believe in the partaking of spirits. I'm glad you're not one of those types. I was a little concerned because you see John a lot, and I know he runs that bar downtown."

"Oh! That…I just like playing checkers with some of the old timers…doing research, you know…historic stuff for the book…. Getting lots of good material from the ancient guys!"

She looked me in the eyes and at once, her shyness faded. Her eyes blazed flashes of color that were instantly gone. Then they were normal. I had never seen eyes like that before. They transmitted a current of airborne electric energy that left me tingling.

"That's a big relief…knowing that's all it is. Goodnight again."

"Yes, goodnight again."

I jumped in the car and turned the lights on so she could see her way up the walk. In the headlights, I could see gutters sagging, a few cracked windowpanes, the porch steps were uneven. I noticed she had to nudge the door with her knee, because it seemed to hang on the threshold. She disappeared inside. As I backed up, I saw a faint glowing light flickering to life in the house.

The poor thing, I thought—no electricity, and the place would be falling down around her if she didn't get some help soon. It was beyond my wildest imagination. She needed my help. My racing mind began the plan as I drove home.

Chapter 9

I got up early the next day.

I had told Leilauna that I didn't drink.

Now, I may seem like an untruthful player, but most of my head-speak is just my insecurity coming out. I really haven't had monumental luck with women. Long-term relationships just never seem to work out with me. So ever since being divorced some years back, I have taken my lumps in the singles life. Some of them because I swore off of marriage a long time back. That was *before* I got divorced.

I've never been a drinker of hard liquor, but I do love to slurp a few beers. Last night I took the pledge.

I had decided that for me to have an honest chance with Leilauna, I would have to be honest. I had given up drinking. Now I had thought about it many times over the years. The older I got, the more absurd the idea seemed. Yet here, waking bright and early without the usual sluggishness, I thought there might be some great benefits of not succumbing to the pull.

Well I sat down and wrote the beginning ten pages of the Mussel Shoals book. It was great! I was so excited I read it three times while doing some polishing.

I ate a quick sandwich and some soup. Mimi had made a handsome stack of them, so I let her pack me a few for later. I was going down to John's to write some more. He would probably eat the ones I didn't.

If the clientele were absent, I would confide in him about my previous evening.

John was the kind of guy who would keep a secret if you asked him for his word on the matter. He had become my unofficial shrink, and we understood that things between us were *just* between us. I was on a top-secret mission. I needed some tactical support.

I ended up at John's place just after one. Usually the checkers crowd was home for their afternoon siesta, and the place would be deserted at that time.

Opening the door, John was sitting behind the bar as usual. I had never seen him drink, but when I came in there was an open beer sitting in front of him.

I sat down across from him, and he shoved the beer towards me.

"You are being a bit presumptuous, don't you think?" I said, looking at the can.

"You don't want it?"

John picked up the can and drank it without stopping. I watched his big adam's apple bobbing with each glug. I was wishing my own adam's apple were doing that familiar dance. I felt a longing, kind of like homesickness my first time at summer camp. Something so familiar was out of my reach. My hand clenched a non-existent can that was *not* sitting on the bar. It was like phantom pains felt in the armless stub of someone who has lost a limb.

John set down the empty can. "I wasn't being presumptuous. Every time you've walked through that door, the first thing you do is ask for a beer or open the beer I have on the bar for you. It would be presumptuous for me to think you didn't want one."

He had a point there.

"Are you turning over a new leaf?" He didn't stop, since I hadn't replied immediately. I was thinking...about having a beer, my oath, and will power, honor, and a myriad of complexities I had not had issues with before.

"I don't care if you don't drink when you come in here… the checkers club hardly touch the stuff. I don't need your money, Jay. You are entertaining to talk to though. I get way more value outta your sorry ass stories than anything else." He rumbled a chuckle. "What are you up to today?"

"I have to find some used carpentry tools, some paint brushes, and a ladder."

"You planning to carry all that around in your rental car, Jay?" He smiled again.

"I hadn't really thought about that."

"Well rumor has it that ole Ben the handyman is retiring. He has a nice old truck and all the tools. Lots of 'em are old, but he's only asking forty-five hundred for the package."

"Forty-five hundred?" That was more than half of what I had budgeted for my summer get-away in Mussel Shoals.

"Yeah, well that includes all his longtime customers."

"I don't want the customers! I *might* be interested in the truck and tools. Where could I find him?"

"About this time of day, he'd probably be down river, at the old sawmill dock fishin'."

"Thanks, John."

I turned to leave, and he said, "What the hell has gotten into you?"

"I'll tell you later," I said, as I walked out.

Chapter 10

THE OLD SAW mill road was full of potholes with depths unknown. I should have rented a Jeep, I thought, as I heard the underside of the car scrape something that sounded like big, rough rocks.

I could see the dock ahead, so I kept going, figuring backing up would only make it worse.

There was an old army green canvas strung up on some spars. I saw three men sitting in the shaded area. All of them had fishing poles.

There was one vehicle parked and it was a panel truck, the vintage and make was a mystery to me, but the thing was in pretty fair shape. I would have to get rid of the lettering on the side, or maybe not. Being undercover as a handy man might be quite handy. The lettering made it an official business. Who would suspect differently?

I parked the rental car and walked out on the dock, quickly calculating the monthly rental payment along with taxes. If I stayed in Mussel Shoals for the entire summer, I would have paid over half the asking price for the panel truck and tools. I was here for some serious negotiating. I hoped the old boy had eaten his Wheaties.

The three of them looked at me like I was the most interesting thing that had happened all day. I noticed that the fishing poles these guys used were short and stout. There was a rowboat in the water. It was tied next to a rickety old ladder.

Looking out on the water, I saw several large Styrofoam bowties floating. Around them was wrapped line, lots of big heavy line. I had never seen fishing like that.

The water here was unlike most I'd seen in the area. It was fairly clear and looked good to swim in, unlike the mud that passed for water everywhere else I'd seen locally.

I was the first to speak, since these guys didn't seem too talkative. "Hi there. I'm Jay," I said. "John said that I could find Ben down here and that his truck and tools were for sale."

"I'm Ben. You interested?"

"I might be. How much are you asking?"

"Fifty-five hundred for the package: panel truck, tools, and clientele."

"John said he thought you wanted forty-five."

"Well I was askin' forty-five, but the boys and me, we been here talkin' and adding up the tools and the income and all the repairs I done to the truck, and we decided forty-five was too low."

I stood in silence, appraising the three. Here I was figuring I would be able the get the old guy down to about three thousand, and he was up near six already. "I'm not interested in the clientele, just the truck and tools. You're welcome to sell your client list to some other local handyman."

That should be good for a couple thousand off, I thought confidently.

"Well now, let's see…I could probably get five hundred from someone wanting a little more business, but it would be a tough sell. Okay, I guess I could take an even five thousand."

I really don't want to admit what I paid old Ben, but to make a long story short, it was a lot more than I wanted to.

I had to dip into my off-limits retirement account to make the transaction fly. But now I was a full-fledged handyman. I just needed to get some how-to books so I could get to work.

The panel truck was a '52 Ford. It had a more modern 300 six-cylinder that had been recently rebuilt. Ben had kept immaculate maintenance records. I felt sure if I drove the old thing up north somewhere when I was finished fixing up Leilauna's farm, I could sell it without the tools for what I'd paid for the entire package.

I pulled Ben and his friends away from fishing and had them drive the truck to Mimi's. Then I dropped them off at Ben's house, where he had another vehicle. The whole deal had taken less than an hour. Fortunately, Ben took a personal check. I was awestruck by the trust these southern folk held for their fellow man.

I drove back to Mimi's, parked the rental car, and jumped into my new business vehicle on my way to see John.

I was excited. The rig didn't have air conditioning, so I just rolled down the windows, opened the rooftop vent, and cruised. I felt like I was one of these people now. No longer did I stick out like a green avocado amongst a box of ripe ones. I was really getting into the southern groove.

For all I knew, this panel truck had been around town when Mussel Shoals was really happening. I started imagining the history of the vehicle, all the places it had been and all the repairs it had seen through.

There was a small problem. The thing had only one seat. Ben had removed the passenger seat, so he could haul healthy quantities of long lumber and such things that handymen have to haul.

I figured I could pick up another seat at a local junkyard and have it installed by the time Leilauna was on her evening walk home.

John's place was just ahead. I shut off my very vivid imagination and set my sights on getting some strategic advice on how I should manage myself and how I could make sure Leilauna's snow white reputation could be protected at all cost.

No one but John was in the bar. I walked up and sat down across from him. This time he hadn't pulled a beer out for me. I was glad. It had been over twenty-four hours since I'd had one. I didn't need my willpower tested at this point.

"Hey, John. How's it hangin'?"

He ignored my greeting. "What are you, out for a test drive?" He was looking in disbelief at my new ride.

"I bought it! Thanks for hooking me up. Perfect timing!"

Big John started that deep rumbling chuckle. "Shit man, I thought this handyman thing was just another one of those little boy fantasies—it would disappear as quick as it came upon you. I thought you was here to write a book. Now you going into the fix-up business? You think a bunch of southern folk gonna hire a Yankee to do their fixing?" He smiled after he quit the chuckle and looked at me like this was some great big practical joke.

"I *am* here to write a book. For your information, I finally got it started this morning. I banged out ten gorgeous pages. Hey man, you don't mind if I use you as one of the characters, do you?"

"Will it put this place on the map? Will it bring more people in here?" he asked, looking real stern and serious.

"I hardly think so. How would they ever find the place? You aren't in the yellow pages, and I would never have noticed that miserable little sign of yours except I was in that intense scouting mode I hit when I'm thirsty and need a beer. Besides," I added, "if you were really worried you could ditch the canary yellow. A tan color would match the plywood better and make the sign almost invisible."

He looked cerebral for a moment and then said, "You know, I was hesitant about the yellow. Maybe I *should* change the color. After all, *you* found this place."

He said "you" like I was retarded or something. John had a way of humbling people. He did it to me all the time. My head had shrunk a couple hat sizes since coming to Mussel Shoals. It was a characteristic imbedded intrinsically into his personality. It made me like him more each time he managed it.

Getting back to the truck, I said, "I don't want a bunch of fix-it business." I shut up, leaving the thought dangling. John's intense curiosity was one of the things I liked toying with. I got some satisfaction from him wanting to know something I was intentionally keeping from him. He had unsureness written on his face. My ploy had worked.

"All right…you playin' wit' me…. He reached across his pallet bar and grabbed me by the collar with one hand. I felt my feet come off the ground and I said, "Okay! Okay! But you've got to promise to keep it all between us." I looked furtively from side to side to see that no old checker playing fossilized spies had emerged silently from the restroom. Satisfied we were alone, I began my desperate story about my infatuation with Leilauna, as John set me back down.

When I finished laying out my plan of conquest, John looked at me with a deep, overriding sympathy. It looked like a little pity as well.

"You mean to tell me you plan on going up there and slaving for that young thing, *hoping* desperately she will soften and *not* see your sorry old ass for what it is?"

Another half a hat size, I could feel my head shrinking as he spoke. A few more sentences and I would look like Pee-wee Herman.

"In a nutshell, yes. But I also have my greatest secret weapon. You are not even considering that!"

"What, may I ask, is that? Whatever you do, don't start unzipping your fly, else I'll throw you right outta here."

"You, John, have overlooked the most powerful tool in my handyman arsenal."

"What pray tell would that be?"

"My personality!"

Big John started laughing. He didn't quit for some time. When he did, he apologized.

"Man, I…I'm sorry…It's just…that…now that *was* funny! I can see you have your heart set on making a complete fool out of yourself," he said. "I won't be the one to stop you."

"What do you mean?"

"Don't you think that young thing is playing you?"

"Of course not! She steadfastly refused my help! I had to promise…oh! I almost forgot…John…this all has to stay just between us. I would commit suicide if she found out I told anyone. She made me promise to keep me helping her, a secret…if she decides I can help."

He looked at me without speaking. I thought at first I saw disdain in his eyes, but then they softened. "Yeah…I promise. You mean she hasn't said yes?"

Then he added something that frightened me. He said, "Ain't no secrets in Mussel Shoals, Jay. Just thought I better warn you. If your secret handyman work gets on the lazy Susan of local gossip, it won't be me that put it there."

"Thanks, John!" His words went in my ears and up in a smoke plume created by the fire of my determination.

I knew I could pull off my secret mission. It wasn't that I thought I could do the work without anyone knowing. I did believe, however naïve it might have been, that my *actual* agenda would be so well cloaked beneath paint, sawdust, and plumbing grime that no one would be the wiser. Except John, I reminded myself.

"Man," he said, "she's got you by the short hairs already, and you ain't been in town a week. Do you think just because you go on up there and slave away for her that she's going to let you in her pants?"

"She doesn't wear pants, John. She's real old-fashioned. Besides, I slaved for my ex-wife for a decade and a half. In the end…she got more than half of everything, even though she never had a job! If I add up the times she graced me with sex after our first year of wedded bliss, then got out a calculator and divided the dollars by acts of intimacy, the price would stagger your sheltered mind!"

He just shook his big head. "Man you are pitiful!"

"I won't argue. Can I lay out my plan? I need your advice."

"Yeah," he said, looking tired.

"You see, I'm not from around here. I don't know local protocol. I don't want to cause Leilauna any problems. Could you just lay out some ground-rules for me? You know, some Deep South etiquette for being around a young, single, Sunday school teacher?"

I had beseeched him desperately. If he was the true friend I felt he was, he would level with me and impart truth in a nutshell.

"You are playing with fire, Jay!"

"Is that it? That's all you have for me? I thought we were friends! Don't leave me hanging without a shred of hope."

"All right man," he said, shaking his head. "It's your funeral."

Those words rung in my mind as he explained the basics. Work hours were nine to five. Nothing past dark. No having her accompany me to the builder's supply, and most importantly, never be seen alone with her in her bedroom.

"That's it?" I asked. It was all so simple.

"That's the basics, man, but you're way out of your league."

"Hey, I grew up in the city. We used to skip school and take the bus downtown when I was in eighth grade. I can take care of myself."

"This is Mussel Shoals, Jay. It's not Seattle. You're in a whole other dimension! Want a beer?"

"Naw. I gave it up."

John looked at me in surprise, then said, "What a man will do…. You think that chameleon act is going to work?"

"John…she asked if I drank alcohol. I knew if I said yes, the deck would be stacked against me! What was I supposed to do?"

"How about tellin' the truth?"

"I did, John. I don't drink anymore."

John paused for a long moment while looking steadfastly at me.

"To tell you the truth, Jay, I like you better already."

His words were the most important of the day.

Needing some reassurance, I asked, "Do you mean it?"

"Get outa here! You better go and sharpen your saw. Do you even know how to sharpen a saw?"

"No…I just figured if it was dull, I would buy a new one."

"That ain't all you'll be buying! Get outa here now! I got enough to think about without you laying all these demented, childlike fantasies on me."

Chapter 11

I KNEW JOHN was silently rooting for me. In his mind, the odds of success were the frozen side of bleak. In mine, they were borderline between good and exceptional. He just didn't want me getting my hopes up only to have them dashed upon the crags of reality. That's the difference between John and me—he is a realist, and I'm opportunistic. Hey, if it knocks on your door, you'd better open it.

I jumped in my rig and set off to the junkyard for a passenger's seat. They had lots of seats already pulled out, so I bought one that felt comfortable. It was tough to get in the side door, so I finally carried it in through the back doors. Problem solved. The seat wasn't mounted, but it was getting late.

Leilauna looked over her shoulder as she heard the panel van come from behind. I saw what looked like satisfaction beam in her eyes for a second when she saw me behind the wheel.

I was almost stopped when she opened the door and jumped in conspiratorially. I laughed, then realized it wasn't completely a joke.

Her driveway came up and I made the turn. We had seen no other cars. We had made it undiscovered.

As we drove up the hill, I said frankly, "People are bound to see you riding with me. Best if you tell them you found a bunch of material in the barn and my labor is affordable because I'm retired."

She looked at me, and her face softly brightened. "That makes perfect sense. Gram could have left me a little cache, just enough to pay some labor."

"Well, here we are." I announced the obvious to mask the more heartfelt.

"Thanks again for the ride, Jay!"

"So I was thinking I could show up in the morning and make a list of some of the repairs so I can get supplies."

"I know there are a few things in the barn. We should see what all is in there, make a list of it. Say around nine am?"

"Sounds perfect! I look forward to it."

She started up the walk towards the house. It was almost dark, but I could still see her move fluidly away. Then she stopped and said excitedly, "Oh! I almost forgot. I found a little place. It's furnished and not far away, over in the next little valley. Maybe we could look at it tomorrow? I have a key."

"Sounds wonderful! Goodnight!"

She waved and scampered up the walk, towards my new job.

I was on the job at nine am the next morning.

I had never seen Leilauna in jeans before, although she'd grown up on this farm and probably wore jeans all the time. Her hair was pony-tailed, and she looked all business. The jeans were…shall we say snug, her heavenly proportions framed in denim. I was the discerning art critic, admiring, imagining….

Going into the barn a couple of owls flew out. "You know the local Indians say that when you are with someone you like a lot, and you both see a pair of owls in daylight, it's a good omen."

"Really? I like the sound of that," I said, focusing in on the words, "like a lot." We walked through the barn to the back, and she opened a big door. Light flared in, illuminating the dust motes in the air and a big, dirty old tarp covering a large pile of something. I figured it would be manure or hay.

We drug the dusty thing off, and underneath was a virtual treasure trove of building materials from lumber to gutters, an assortment of nails, paint, and other useful stuff.

"Wow, your grandma *was* planning to do the repairs. She just didn't get to it," I said.

"Maybe she ran out of money and couldn't finish all the projects she'd planned."

"Yeah probably," I answered, thinking rapidly. I had planned to pick up my how-to manuals on my first trip to the builder's supply. Here *was* the builder's supply, only with no manuals.

"Well, let's go take a look around the old place and—"

"Jay?"

"Yes?"

"You know I said my foot went through the floor of the barn, where I milk the cow? Maybe that would be a good place to start."

"Great idea! Let's go take a look. I'll follow you."

If I could just follow her around for a few minutes every hour, I would be content. Being behind this woman was something extraordinary. My heart sailed into the sky; my eyes followed the bewitching motions of her form.

It was a bank barn, built into the side of the hill. The milking area was elevated above the lower level. It was an area big enough to hold five or so cows. I could tell from the stalls. I could see daylight coming up from a few holes in the wooden floor.

"Do you think we should patch it, Jay...or do you think *all* the planks need replacing?"

"Looks to me like most of them are so worn they are weak. The whole thing should be re-done."

"That's kind of what I was thinking. I'm glad we think alike."

She looked me in the eyes. Hers were so warm, so innocent. I said, self-consciously, "Well, I'll go get some similar lumber and get started."

"I can help you load it."

"Sure, if you want to."

She was really something. She pitched right in as well as any man would have. I drove around the barn and backed in near the work area. There was a lot of manure to move before I could get to the rotten planks, so I just dug in and she helped with the wheelbarrow and shoveling. With two of us working together as a team, the crap really flew.

Next, I took a couple of crowbars from my truck and commenced to tearing the old floor out. I replaced it as I went so that I could use the old pieces as a rough pattern. The stalls came apart pretty easily, and as soon as I had new floor down, I rebuilt them so I could use the others as a plan.

By lunch time, I had one stall reassembled and the floor for the next one complete. This was looking like a dirty, grueling, three-day job.

Leilauna brought some lunch, along with a bucket of hot water and a towel. We went into the sunlight and I cleaned up. She looked simply irresistible with the golden light playing and highlighting pieces of her dark hair. Her tanned skin was lightly flushed by the physical exertion. I could just imagine….

"Jay, perhaps we should take a break and go look at the little house I found. You have been working so hard. The floor looks great, by the way. Thanks so much for helping. I was honestly afraid to go in that area of the barn since my accident. I feel so much better now."

She took a deep breath, gave a long sigh, and looked up through the green leaves. Filtered sunlight dappled her face. In that moment, I fell in love.

Now I know that we had just met, and I really knew very little of her personality, other than that she was a hard worker, thoughtful, complimentary, and kind. What more could a man want? I thought, as I munched on a sandwich. I wanted to erase more of her fears. The barn floor would take care of one. I wondered how many more she might have.

I thought for a moment about the side trip to the house she had found, deciding instantly.

"If you don't mind, Leilauna, I would like to keep moving on the barn floor. I am just getting my rhythm and think we could get a third of it done today if we stick with it."

I didn't want her thinking I was one of those citified pansies who could only work a half day. No! I was the handyman and was chomping at the bit to show her what I could accomplish in a *full* day.

"How about we go to the house when it gets hot? It's still pretty cool inside the barn. We could clean up and take the drive later in the afternoon."

"Whatever you want, Jay."

Those words took my brain to heights of which I had not dreamed. The sound of them echoing in my affection-starved mind made me smile a larger, more genuine smile than I had experienced for the longest time. My face felt like it might crack, and muscles were strained into positions they weren't used to.

"Have you ever used a chop saw?" I asked.

"No, never."

"Well, it is really easy. You see...I can teach you. If I mark the planks and you chop them to length, we could get the job done much faster."

"Jay, I will do anything to make your work easier. Just give me a quick lesson."

We went back into the barn, and I drew a line on a plank and, making sure she wore safety glasses, put a plank on the saw and said, "Okay, stand here in front of me, and I'll show you how to cut it just right."

I first showed her how to align the plank with the cutting path of the blade. That necessitated me standing very close behind her and placing my hand on hers.

There was that electricity again.

I had a hard time focusing on the task. Her scent, the sweet smell of her womanly form, mixed with perspiration and I guess her shampoo, made my already flooding mind reel.

We cut a couple of planks together. I finished the lesson and hung in place.

"I think I've got it, Jay."

She glanced over her shoulder at me. I was distracted by her gaze. I felt the slightest brush of her bottom against me. Then in a flash, it was gone. I couldn't tell if it was a signal to move...even though she *had* said the cutting was under control.

The thought of her being so close kept me working like a banshee all afternoon.

When the heat became unbearable, and I was exhausted from so much physical exertion, we gave it up. I was soaked through with sweat and covered in a dark greenish black sludge that could only be one of the things I hate the most—excrement.

She was perspiring evenly all over, but clean. A little sawdust rested on her shoulders. Her sweet scent wafted towards me.

I had brought a change of clothes, planning to visit the little house she had found. I just didn't know how to bring up changing, or where to do it.

"Jay, we can't go out looking like this. We are drenched. I must stink like a herd of cattle! Come. Did you happen to bring a change of clothes?"

"Yes, I was planning on changing before we went out. And for your information, I think you smell wonderful."

"You are a sick man, Jay VanVessey! I reek. I can hardly stand myself. Get your clothes and wait here. I'll be just a minute."

She was back in a flash. She carried a wicker basket. I could see towels. This should be interesting, I thought. Anticipation rammed its way through my brain like a bullet train derailing. I was overwhelmed and just decided not to over think things. In Alabama, you just go with the flow. I was feeling more southern all the time.

She walked up and broke out that award-winning smile again. "I don't really have a decent bathroom. It needs some repairs. I have to heat water on the woodstove and take sponge baths."

I was picturing her standing in a galvanized tub full of bubbles.

"Up on the ridge though, is a very special place. I don't take anyone there because I don't want others to know it exists. It is kind of my sacred spiritual place. I feel close to you, Jay. You are so generous and kind. I don't think I've ever met a man who is so thoughtful and considerate."

She handed me another sandwich, and we walked up the hill on a well-worn trail through a mixed forest of southern pine and a variety of hardwoods. Before long, the trail broke out of the timber and into a small clearing. There was a small stream that disappeared underground. It was like finding a ray of sunlight on your shoulders when nothing but clouds seem to fill the sky.

She looked back at me and motioned for me to follow. Stepping on limestone shelves, we walked upward for about a hundred yards and then there was an unbelievable pool carved in the rock. A good-sized flow of clear water ran out of a cleft in the limestone and into the pool.

"Wow! I never would have thought!"

"My granddad made this reservoir. Our family homesteaded this land because of this spring. My great-great-grandfather found it. My granddad drilled and dynamited this pool out of the limestone. He used the rock from it for the foundations of the barn you and I are working on.

"So you see why I want to bring the farm back? I don't want it going the way so many places do down here. You know...people don't care how much work their ancestors put into a place they may have inherited. It breaks my heart to see so many of the great old barns and houses falling down for lack of care. Why most people just bring in a mobile home and move out of their ancestral home, I have no idea!"

I could see emotion building behind her gorgeous, luminous and immense brown eyes. It seemed as though they were swallowing me. This was a woman with family values, I thought.

"Jay...I don't have a swim suit," she said, changing the subject. "I normally come here alone. I do have my underwear, which are no more revealing. Do you think that it would be okay...I mean, if I got into the water like that?"

"By all means. I don't have any trunks with me either," I told her. "I just have my briefs."

"Well…maybe you should turn around while I get in the water, okay?"

I was heartbroken but agreed without flinching. To see this heavenly creature disrobe before my very eyes… she was probably right, the wise decision and all. I turned around and before long heard a splash, then her voice saying, "Oh! The water is so nice. You can turn around now."

Her voluminous hair was floating on the surface, flowing out around her face, framing it in a wondrous play of dark, undulating strands. The crystal water shone through the strands as they saturated and began to sink.

I was mesmerized. I was standing frozen in place, indelibly inscribing the sight into the vault of my memory forever to come. Even in my next life, I thought, this memory would follow me. It was the most spectacular of my entire forty-six years.

She laughed and said, "Jay, you look like you've seen a ghost. Are you okay?"

"Never better." I had not dared to speak words of affection to her. I was being cautious. At this moment, a torrent of thoughts were fighting to drop onto my tongue. I said only, "Leilauna, you look heavenly right now. I mean *more* so than usual."

She caught me glancing beneath the surface and she checked, making sure none of her very ample bodily features had slipped from their containments. She blushed slightly, beneath her beautiful brown hair, and said, sounding a little flustered, "Get in, silly!"

I took off my shirt, shoes, and jeans and climbed in. She had averted her eyes until I was in the water. It was wonderful, and I said so.

"I love this place. If it weren't for this spot, the farm would be just like so many other run-down places. When I come home, though, I don't see the dilapidation. I see what it will be someday. Thanks for helping me, Jay."

She swam over to me, and in a movement so quick I almost missed it by blinking, she pecked my cheek. An instant later, she was back on the other side of the pool.

The water was cool, but not cold. It was refreshing and quickly brought my boiling blood back into a safe zone.

She asked if I could reach the shampoo. I turned and rose slightly out of the water to reach it. When I turned back towards her, I saw her watching me. She quickly shifted her eyes away. For a moment, I thought I'd seen a flash of longing within them, but I couldn't be sure.

We bathed and splashed and acted like a couple of overgrown kids. Finally, with the sun dropping into the western sky, she sighed and said, "We should get going if you want to see the house in daylight."

I agreed, reluctantly, and she climbed from the water. This time she said nothing about me turning away, so I didn't.

Leilauna was not a small woman. She was of average height. I was struck by her tiny waist. She was what many would call full-figured, but her curves were exaggerated because of the drastic sweep from her well-endowed chest and hips narrowing down to an extraordinarily small waistline. Her form actually took my breath away.

As she climbed from the water, she had to bend at the waist. I had died and gone to heaven. I would gladly sweat and slave daily for a glimpse of her in that position. My knees were weak, so I stayed in the water while she quickly wrapped a towel around herself.

"You'd better hurry, Jay," she said. "The sun will be down soon." She looked at me quizzically. I must have had a look on my face that showed all the yearning pounding inside my feeble brain. "Yes...yes...I'll get out now."

She turned, allowing me to wrap a towel around myself. Then she said, "I'll run to the house and change. You should probably do the same here. It wouldn't do for some wandering hunter to see you walking through *my* woods wrapped in a towel."

"Sure," I said, speechless, wondering how many wandering hunters there were lurking about these parts.

"Oh, and Jay. Please don't speak a word of this...I mean of us bathing, or of this spot to anyone. Not even to John. Will you promise me that?"

"I promise," I said, without even thinking. Her wish had become my command.

Chapter 12

We climbed into the old Ford and drove away from town and up the hill on the blacktop. A mile or two away, there was a right turn, and Leilauna directed me to take it. This was a part of Alabama I had never imagined. There were streams bubbling down verdant hillsides, and the air had cooled as we climbed to a little higher elevation.

After a time she said, "Turn right here." There was no mailbox or any other indicator of this being a road to a domicile. I began wondering what those wandering hunters shot in these woods. If I were to be up here by myself...in dueling banjo country, it might be a good idea to purchase a gun.

I looked to her, as my overactive mind ran the most cynical scenarios, and she was all smiles.

Just then, an idyllic little house came into view. It had cedar shake siding and a tin roof. It looked to be well maintained and was set back against the hill. The forest ran nearly up to the back door. There was a small hand-hewn barn down in a lower field.

"Well, what do you think?" she asked.

"I feel like I've stepped back in time about a hundred years. It's great! Does it have indoor plumbing?"

She looked at me, kind of embarrassed. I felt immediately that I had said the wrong thing.

"Yes, Jay, it's very comfortable with electricity, a flush toilet, hot water, a tub, and shower."

She sighed. "I'm sorry my place is so primitive. Most people don't live that way around here. My Gram was kind of old fashioned and didn't adapt to the modern changes as fast as some other people. She refused steadfastly to hook up to the power grid, saying it was just another way the government had of getting into your pocket book.

"She was a dear old thing, but stubborn as a mule. When she had her mind set on something, you couldn't change her course with dynamite."

Leilauna was introspective for a time, and we sat in comfortable silence taking in the view as the sunset's colors played on the fields and forest.

"I guess I'm a lot like her in some ways," she said. "We were very close; living together for so long and all. Sometimes I think she loved me more than my own mother."

This was the first time I had learned much of anything about Leilauna's family. We had just begun our friendship. I looked forward to learning more of her personality and family.

"Let's go in!" she said. Without waiting, she threw the truck door open and bounded up the two front steps. I got out and followed far enough behind to get a good picture of the place—and of her.

Opening the door, we walked in. I expected to smell the closed up scents of a place unused for a time. I was surprised that it had a very homey, lived-in smell. Wood smoke and cooking had permeated the dwelling.

I thought of its history and what it could say if the walls spoke.

The place had one good-sized bedroom and another smaller one that looked west out over the field and barn. "Leilauna, it's great! This room will make a perfect writing space. I love the view. And it's so close to your place. How much do they want for it?"

I had looked around a bit and knew that a place in a good area, well maintained with acreage, would fetch a tidy dollar. I was prepared to spend a considerable sum for the convenience of being in such close proximity to the woman of my dreams. I braced myself for the bad news.

"Would three twenty-five a month be too much? I mean this house is in a family trust, and they really don't need to rent it."

I stopped myself just short of gasping. I was paying a grand a month at Mimi's. Of course, that included food and her company, but three twenty-five for this?!

I recovered nicely, saying, "No, that is right in my budget. Are you sure the price is correct? There is not some mistake? It seems so reasonable."

I caught the slightest mischievous twinkle in her eyes as she said, "Three twenty-five, that's it. Of course you have to pay the electric and put it in your name."

"Where do I sign?"

"I can get the paperwork tomorrow at church. If you want to give me the money, I'll set it all up!"

"You are a dream, Leilauna."

She literally beamed.

I was ecstatic but tried not to let it show.

Chapter 13

ONE THING I can say about John is that he's dedicated. I found out early on that his hours were one in the afternoon until nine in the evening. He would lock up early once in a while when the checkers club wasn't in session.

I knew John would be disappointed if I didn't stop in and visit after my first day as a handyman. I was not going to gloat, or talk about anything but work. That was enough. I was offering him the opportunity to pry into my personal life. I chuckled, thinking of how he would approach the subject.

John's place had a few of the old guys at the checkers table, so I sat on the far end of the bar, which was unusual for me. I normally sat right in front of where John kept the beer, so that his big frame wouldn't have to heave one way or the other.

He noticed as soon as I had made my turn away from the pit stop. He discreetly pointed with is thumb to the beer as he was going by, and I shook my head. The floor gave up some grief under John's bulk. He made his way around the end of the bar and plopped on a stool next to me, effectively erasing me from the sights of the old guys.

"So, how was your first day of work?"

"Oh, it was a shit job," I said. "We mucked out part of the barn and tore up the floor. Then we started laying the new one back down and rebuilt two stalls. It was a long day. I'm beat. I must have drunk a gallon of water I sweated so much."

"Mhhmm.... That's pretty hard work...pretty dirty, too!"

He looked at my clothes, and I knew....

"Yeah, Mimi called and said she made dinner, but you never showed."

"When was that, John?"

"About five minutes ago. Now, you want to tell me what you've been up to?"

John looked at me in a way I had seen before. The most memorable was when my feet were off the ground. I knew stretching the truth was out of the question. So I just left a little of it out.

"Well we worked late. I got a third of the floor ripped out and replaced and then rebuilt two stalls. Of course, I couldn't have done it without her help. She is amazing!"

"I know she is, Jay...so why you so late?"

"Oh, we had a bite to eat and cleaned up and then she took me to a little farm, and I rented it."

"You did what?"

"I rented a place for the summer. I can't write at Mimi's."

"Wait a minute. You told me yesterday that you had done ten...what was it you said...ten gorgeous pages?"

"Well, yeah! I did, but that was the first good work I've done in a week. A writer can't survive on that kind of production."

"You sound like you're building Oldsmobiles or something!" He shook his head. "Anyway...where did you get cleaned up?"

"Oh!.... She's got a spring on the place. Nice clear water, too."

"Yeah, you look good and clean. Where did you change clothes?"

This was the third degree. I knew complying with John's questioning was the only option. Maybe it was because he was older than me, or wiser, or so much bigger.

"In the woods."

"Where in the woods?" The questions were closing in on the mark.

"By the spring."

"You was at the dynamite hole?"

"Yes."

"With her?"

"Yes."

John was speechless for a while. He turned his face away. I couldn't see his expression. All I saw were those big inner tubes...I mean the back of his neck going side to side.

When he turned to face me, he possessed a look of bewilderment. He spoke softly, and I could see it was really difficult for him.

"What do you think you're doing? Didn't I tell you nine to five only?"

"Well yes, that was for work. We went to see the house after work."

"Yes, Jay. That is a grey area. I should have known you would push the envelope! But are you kidding me? You were at the dynamite hole...with her?"

I nodded.

John said, "Her church don't allow men and women swimming together, Jay...tell me you went there but swam separately."

I could tell Big John wanted to hear that lie, the one almost ready to drip off my tongue, when I said, "We were appropriately dressed. We swam together."

"Don't tell me more. I don't need pictures of Leilauna in a swimming suit. She is hard to get off the mind fully dressed! *Are you crazy?*"

He mouthed the last three words, but I got the picture just the same.

I didn't answer. I thought about a warm beer. I almost caved. The pressure was getting to me. I re-took my vow—for the woman I loved.

Chapter 14

I DROVE UP to Leilauna's the next morning, and we started back on the barn floor. She was as helpful as ever, but when two in the afternoon hit, she said we were done for the day.

We headed up the hill for what was quickly becoming our ritual swim. I had never been happier. I followed her all the way, keeping a close eye on her from behind. I mean, there are poisonous snakes in these parts, and I was keeping an eye out for danger. That's a better way of saying it.

She didn't say anything about me watching. So I watched her strip. This time though, she had on one of those tasteful one-piece bathing suits. It was black and set on her just right.

"I found this in some of my mother's old stuff. It's pretty out of style, but—"

"It looks great on you! You shouldn't make excuses for yourself, Leilauna. You have nothing to be ashamed of. You are the most surprising woman I've ever met."

"Surprising? How?"

"Well for one thing, you are absolutely gorgeous. You're a hard worker, generous, and good spirited…."

"Go on, Jay. I don't mind being flattered."

"I feel so fortunate to have met you…sometimes when I look at you, I get weak in the knees."

"Why do you feel like that?"

"Well because you are just the kind of woman I would be looking for if I were a bit younger."

"Your age looks good to me, Jay." She paused for a moment, then said, "You know, Jay, our pastor doesn't believe in men and women swimming together. He says there is too much temptation. What do you think?"

She was sitting on the limestone; her legs below her knees were dangling in the water. When she asked me the question, she straightened one leg and brought it up level with the surface and just above. It was poised above the water, dripping, like an artist's conceptualization of a woman's perfect leg. I looked at that leg and struggled tearing my eyes away from it.

Then I looked her in the eyes and fibbed a little. "I don't really know what your pastor is talking about. The human body is nothing to be ashamed of. A lot of people lack self-control, I guess." She lowered the leg and brought the other one up in the same fashion.

"Are you one of those people, Jay?"

"Not me," I said. "I'm the picture of self-control. You have nothing to worry about from me...no sir!"

"That's good because I really like coming here with you."

She slid into the water and moved nearer. "Come on in. You must be really hot after working so hard."

I obeyed, and when I was all in, she was right there with the quick cheek peck once again. "That's just a little thank you for all you're doing. I wish I had more to give...I mean to pay you with."

"Your company is payment enough. I enjoy working with you. I was getting bored playing checkers with those old guys anyway."

"So I beat out the checkers club, did I?"

"Hands down."

She smiled, obviously satisfied.

"Oh! I have the paperwork together for the house. You could sign it when we get down to my place. Will you come in for a snack?"

"I was hoping you would ask me in. We'll be done with the barn tomorrow. We need to pick our next project. I was thinking I should look at the VW. I'll bet I could get it running with a bit of tinkering. Did I tell you I had one?"

She shook her head.

"It was my first car in high school. I did all the work on it myself."

She looked like she was going to kiss me again. I blinked in hope, but nothing happened.

After swimming and cleaning up, we walked back down to her house. She asked me to wait on the front porch until she could get a lantern lighted. She wasn't gone long before she returned, took my hand, and led me in through the open door.

The light cast from the lanterns was warm and glowing. We sat down together, and she uncovered some dishes that would put Mimi's to shame.

"Where did you learn to cook like this?" I asked.

"Gram taught me. She was old fashioned and made everything from scratch."

We ate mostly in silence, and when we were finished, she brought out the shortest rental agreement I had ever read. I signed it and went out to get my checkbook.

When I came back in she said, "Make it out to the Mount Zion Family Trust. That's who you send the checks to. The address is at the bottom of your copy."

That all wrapped up, she handed me a key and said, "You can move in tomorrow if you like."

"I think I will, after work. I want to finish the barn floor tomorrow. Are you up for that?"

"I sure am, Jay."

"Well, I guess I'll see you then."

Walking out to my rig, I thought that it had been the most pleasant evening I could remember for a long time. I hadn't even had a beer.

Chapter 15

WE FINISHED UP the barn floor early the next day. We had developed a system that melded us as a team. Once finished, we stood looking at the work and we both started smiling.

After taking our dip, I asked Leilauna if she would like to come with me to the new house. Earlier, I had checked out at Mimi's and even stopped and bought a few household cleaning items on the way to work. I had my two bags with me and figured I would give the place a quick once over.

She agreed to come, so we piled in and drove over. I got to noticing that there were no houses at all between my new place and hers. We enjoyed the short ride, pulled up, and I thought, *Home!* For the next three months anyway.

I grabbed my supplies out of the back of the Ford, and we walked up the front steps. Unlocking the door, I was immediately struck by the smell. The place exuded squeaky. All the trim and furniture had been dusted and wiped. There were no dead flies in the light fixtures; the toilet and tub were shining.

I looked at her, swept away by her thoughtfulness. I hadn't done a damn thing. In other words, Leilauna had done all this...for me...and the only time she could have done it was last night after I left for home.

"I'm in shock. You cleaned this place last night?"

"Well, it wasn't really dirty. I just tidied up a bit."

"Thanks, Leilauna, you are wonderful."

Something happened right there. I saw a little sparkle in the corner of her eye, and I thought, *She's crying.*

"Are you all right?"

She nodded but looked down. I saw her tremble slightly, and I said, "There, there, it will be okay." I was pulled to her. I embraced her sweet little trembling form and just held her for a while.

After a bit, she said, "Since my Gram died, I have longed for someone to say that to me. She used to call me up and say it when she had nothing else pressing."

We had a moment there. It was a window in time opening, and we both reached through. She had a soft heart; I felt it then, when we touched for those few moments. She broke away softly and said very quietly, "Thanks, Jay. It was nice having you just then."

"Anytime."

"Hey, I'd better be getting back." She had awakened. Reality rocked our worlds. We looked into each other's eyes and something was slightly different.

We talked a bit about the morning's project on the drive back, and said goodnight.

I went home, to my new one, settled in, and wrote some great stuff until past midnight.

I got up early the next morning and went into town for some basic maintenance parts for the bug. I bought filters, spark plugs, contact points, five gallons of fresh gas, oil, and a new battery.

I wanted Leilauna to have a ride. There were times when we were working and needed some small thing. She could run errands, but I needed the Ford tool truck on the worksite.

The bug was charmed. I poured the gas in, primed the carb, changed the filters and oil, stuffed the new battery in quickly, fastened it down, then shut the rear hatch. I was confident. These things were bullet proof.

I jumped in, turned the engine over a few times, pumped the gas, and she caught.

I could tell right off she would run like a charm. The oil wasn't dirty. Gram had taken good care of the old thing.

I pulled it out of the pole shed and ran it up near the house. Leilauna brought out some warm soapy water and a hose and we gave the old girl a good scrubbing.

When we were done, the look on Leilauna's face was priceless. She said, "When I was a little girl, Gram used to keep her looking just like that! When she got old, she just couldn't keep up on things."

She had a wistful look on her face, as if she were seeing haunting memories of treasured times.

"She must have been...irreplaceable," I said.

She nodded and jumped in. "It's about time I took *you* for a ride!"

We drove further upland into rolling meadows and farms that were sparse. "Don't forget to buy your license tabs," I reminded her.

She pulled over and stopped at a wide spot. "This is so great! Do you know how much I love this car?"

I nodded.

She just smiled and headed back the way we had come.

"I looked at that generator, and it's in pretty sad shape," I told her. "I don't know how your grandmother nursed it along all these years. Have you ever heard of hydro-power?"

"Of course, Doctor!"

She could be flippantly funny. It was spontaneous and something I enjoyed immensely.

"Well, then you wouldn't need that old generator. I imagine it's pretty loud."

Chapter 16

THE FARM HAD really not been as bad as things looked. The place had been well maintained over its life, except for the last ten years. We pressure washed and painted the house. I paid the gutter people to come out as a gift to Leilauna. The indoor plumbing was minor. A couple of faucets and new shut-offs and everything worked well.

There was still no hot water. I cut loose with five hundred bucks and bought her an on-demand propane water heater, and a big enough tank that the propane truck would come out. Bang, she had hot water and all she needed.

I ran a hot bath when I finished the installation and insisted she use it right then and there.

The spring supplied way more than we used, so hydro made sense. About twelve hundred feet of three inch pipe, and I was sure I could find a little turbine used on the Internet.

Summer had run well into August. I had the Mussel Shoals book about wrapped. My plan had been to spend the summer here and finish anything that wasn't quite done on the project back in Seattle.

Each time I thought about being gone...I couldn't believe the time had flown so fast.

She would ask me now and then how the writing was going, but we never really discussed my leaving. Leilauna's farm was shaping up. Most of the big projects had been taken care of.

One afternoon, we knocked off early and hiked up the hill to the swimming spot. She had brought along some snacks, which we sat and ate quietly once we were done swimming.

Finally, she broke the silence. "When will you be leaving, Jay?"

"I haven't made up my mind," I said. "I should be heading home soon. The funny thing is...I don't even want to go."

"Why?"

"Because, I'll miss you."

I turned away, not wanting her to realize how difficult it would be for me.

She fell silent and didn't say too much for the rest of the afternoon.

The thought of our new friendship being separated, and of living across the country from one another, put a damper on the afternoon. We were pleasant and cheerful, not wanting to think about it more, but it lingered.

Chapter 17

I WAS AWAKENED by her voice. I would know it anywhere. She spoke in the darkness of my bedroom. "Can I stay with you tonight?"

How she got into the house, I didn't care. I slid over. She was warm and soft, lying in close, with one of her legs over me.

I felt myself coming alive and was immediately self-conscious....

She was a Sunday school teacher after all.

"Sorry." I said, and I rolled away slightly so that she would not be disgusted.

Leilauna grabbed my shoulder abruptly and reefed me towards her and flat onto my back.

"Jay....I have longed for this moment."

Then she was straddling me. I felt her hand grasp...with her forceful touch. I flew into heaven...well it seemed so at the time. I desired to never return from it...I had crossed a threshold that swept me towards bliss, a place belonging solely to Leilauna.

When the sun came up, I remembered. I started, and looked next to me. She was gone...and I wondered if it had been a dream...but there was a strand of her long, wavy dark hair on the pillow.

"Oh! My! God!" I said it out loud. There was irrefutable evidence lying on my...I mean on *her* pillow.

I dressed quickly and went to work early. When I pulled into her driveway, her car was gone. Leilauna had become quite the errand runner. I thought nothing of it, and was just finishing the final touches on the turbine fittings when I heard her car coming up the driveway.

I opened the big gate valve and let loose the water. The thing set to humming beautifully. The battery bank had not been completely dead. The inverter had an automatic shut-off when the batteries were only half drained. As soon as the turbine began to charge, I flipped on a couple of light switches inside.

Leilauna arrived just in time to see them come on.

She jumped out of her bug and stood star-struck at the sight. Then she ran up the steps and gave me her hand. "Jay, I...I...." She looked away, and I could tell she was crying.

"What's wrong, sweetheart?"

"Jay...I'm sorry...for what I did last night...."

"No, don't. You were wonderful. I love you. Don't you see there is nothing wrong with us last night?"

"I went to the church and prayed this morning. I felt so guilty...I asked for forgiveness!"

"There is nothing to forgive. You care about me, and I care about you! We finally let it out. What we shared is something wonderful and happy."

"I *can't* be happy about it, Jay!"

"What are you talking about, Leilauna?"

"We're not married! What we did is a sin! I'm sorry...!" Tears streamed down her face. "Please, I need to be alone. I don't feel like working today. Don't you have some writing to do?"

"Leilauna...just talk with me! I don't want to leave you like this. I'm your friend. I care about you. I love you!"

"Then shouldn't you ask me something?"

"What something?"

"Oh! Just go now...I can't...talk to you right now."

"Okay...okay...I'll check in on you later."

With that emotionally overloaded scene wrapped, she ran into her house.

I was dumbfounded. What something? I kept asking myself. What something did she want me to ask? Then it hit me behind the forehead, and it hit me hard! The something was proposing.

PROPOSING! my mind screamed.

Chapter 18

I HAD SWORN off marriage long before my divorce came to an ugly, festering head. Once the attorneys had lanced the abscess, and drained a good percentage of my liquidity, the wife, who had never held a job, got over half of what was left. The experience was painfully embedded like a long, rusty dagger in my heart.

Fortunately, I was an unpublished author at the time. My wife thought my writing was just a worthless hobby I had taken up, so that I could insist on some uninterrupted quiet time in my own home.

She was partially right. I saw words as wings. The fictional pursuits of my characters allowed me time to escape, flying into a world all my own. I also intended to fly from my then wife, with those same wings, only in *real* life.

I had finally taken flight. I was free and unencumbered. I had no worries about sharing what I had earned by pounding away at my laptop for thousands of hours and doing grueling promotional tours with someone I had grown to despise.

She had signed away her rights to my "hobby" with a scoff and a humorous snort. I used to think that little snort was cute when we were new and I was getting laid every night. Then it all changed. In the end, I felt like strangling that snort. Well enough of that...you see...my aversion to the "M" word is easily explained.

My ring finger has been effectively amputated. It is invisible to me, but not others. Single was my creed, although I really needed a kind woman in my bed most nights. Leilauna was that woman. I knew the truth of the situation. Now I just had to convince her that it was not called sin....

I needed John.

I had visited John regularly the past couple months. But since moving out to the farm, working on Leilauna's place, and writing profusely in the evenings, there hadn't been a whole lot of extra time. I had seen him less and less. Plus I had stayed off the beer—that might be part of it, too.

When I came in, his place was the usual dinnertime slow. The big man saw me and said, "Well, look what the cat drug in. I thought maybe you finished that book of yours and you done gone home without saying goodbye to ole Big John!"

I ignored his comments...this was serious and I wasn't in a laughing mood. "Hey man, what's happening?" I asked. Then I laid it all out for him...everything but her slipping into my bed in the middle of the night. He got the divorce story again, my sworn aversion to marriage, and the feelings between Leilauna and me without any of the physical details.

John didn't say anything for a long time. I mean really long...it was at least three minutes. I could tell he was thinking...when he thought *that* hard, he usually came up with a ball buster. I prepared to cover-up.

"So you ain't leaving something out of this little story... are you?"

I hesitated.

"I mean, like you could have forgotten to enlighten me with an important detail?"

I knew what he was referring to, but could not figure out *how* he knew.

His eyebrows lifted.

I started talking real quickly because I had no desire to hear that cracking sound in his voice again. I had learned at least that much.

"Well see, John, she made me promise…."

"Then don't tell me. I'll guess…you been sleeping with her?"

I whimpered, "Only once."

"Only once, the man says! Boy, I knew you were blonde…but I thought you had *some* sense! Now I be wondering forevermore."

"Okay, John!" I said. "I know this is not good. But how do I go about explaining to her we are doing nothing wrong?"

"By whose standard, Jay?"

"By modern standards!" I said, slightly perturbed that he wasn't immediately on my side…rooting for the home team. Why did John always seem to be like a beacon for consequences? Couldn't he just wish me well? Thoughts darted around inside my mind like a wild pony corralled for the first time.

"Boy, haven't you begun to understand that much of this country is trapped someplace back a hundred years or more? Oh sure, we got cars and planes and all the technology, but that's not what I'm talking about. Old-fashioned religious values are alive and well down here! They're still kickin', and sometimes they be kickin' ass! I just hope it ain't yours, my friend!"

He wasn't finished. "You're sleeping with the Sunday school teacher! Who you thinks gonna get the blame? Her? That delightful and innocent young creature? Or you! A wandering handyman writer who has been working on the poor girl's farm. 'Beast!' I can hear it now."

I turned my ear to the street and listened carefully. "I don't hear anything."

"I was talking figuratively, you moron. Will you get a hold of yourself? This be some serious shit if it gets out. I'm actually surprised that people aren't talking about you two already...well, it *is* harvest time. Most folks are too busy working to spend much time gossiping.

"Just wait come winter though...folks around here take gossip to a higher level when most of the crops are in."

"John, come on, man, break it to me. What are my options? What should I do?"

"If I was in your miserably lucky shoes, I'd marry the girl. You don't, you'll be sorry. I just know. I got a feeling for these things."

"John, I can't! Abolish my sacred oath? Impossible!"

"I'll be sure and close on the day of your funeral...in honor of our friendship."

"That is harsh! It can't be that bad," I moaned.

John just raised his eyebrows again and shrugged his shoulders. He looked like he *had* exaggerated my predicament...at least he looked that way to me.

"You haven't been much help, John!"

"Man, I gave you the best advice I know. You just don't want to hear it! If I was you...I'd already be on my honeymoon."

I walked out of John's place shaking my head.

Chapter 19

I DIDN'T SLEEP at all that night, and she did not come to visit, as I'd hoped she would. I would go to her when it was light enough to see. I would go and console her.

I showed up at our usual start time, and her car was gone for the second morning in a row. I thought about driving down to the church and seeing if she was there, but I figured that would only make matters worse.

I puttered around, not really doing anything productive for an hour or so. I realized when I heard her car coming up the drive that I hadn't come to work. I had come to speak with the woman I loved.

She pulled up, and I could see her red-rimmed eyes from the porch.

She got out of the bug and hesitated, without closing the door. She looked at me like I was a stranger, or like I had bad news to deliver.

She finally shut the car door and walked up. I started down the porch steps and met her on the sidewalk. She let me hug her, but the whole thing was stiff and forced.

"Leilauna, I need to speak with you. Should we go inside?"

"Jay...this is really hard for me to say, but you shouldn't come in. In fact, you should probably leave."

"Leilauna, this is your friend, Jay. We're buddies, workmates. We love each other. Just talk with me! We can sort this out."

"Jay…you come here and say you love me…and it breaks my heart! I'm so torn between right and wrong. I'm confused…I just need some time to adjust to what has happened." She paused for a moment, and then went on. "The night I came to you was wonderful. But when I woke in the morning, I knew it was wrong, that I shouldn't be with you like that because we're not married. That is why I said it was sin."

"Leilauna, I assure you it is not! Jesus preached to love your brother like yourself!"

"But he didn't say you should sleep with your brother, did he?" She smiled, and I saw hope.

"Walk with me, please? Don't just walk away from what we have; it is too precious."

I took her hand and said, "Come, let's go up to the swimming hole. I bet it's real pretty up there in the morning light."

She weakened, and I pulled her at first. The farther we walked, the better we felt. Her smile came back, and it seemed we had gone back a couple days in time, to before…before it had happened.

The morning light played over the water. I pulled off my work boots, rolled up my jeans, and dangled my legs in. She sat down, hiked up her dress, and did the same. I took her hand and we just sat there for a long time, saying nothing.

The water spoke as it ran down from the cleft and into the pool. Right then, it seemed to be the only voice we needed.

Finally, I said, "It's warmer than I thought it would be. Shall we?"

She looked up at me. This was our special place. We had come here nearly every day for the past two months. She nodded without speaking.

I took off my clothes except for my briefs—I wasn't going to break tradition—and got in. She followed. This time though, was unlike the others. Her modesty had departed, and she stripped down to nothing but skin. I watched in awe.

She came to me without hesitation, refracted sunlight playing on her skin. She was a dream. She took me into a dimension I had never before experienced. We became inseparable that day. At least that's the way I felt.

I had been lost. Now I was found. My outlook changed like flicking a light switch. She was mine. We would not be denied.

The next few months went on. I stayed in the little rented farm in Mussel Shoals much longer than I had planned.

She would come to me in the night. We visited the swimming hole nearly every day. We continued detail work on her farm. The big projects were wrapped.

There was still a monumental problem for me; she would never consent to going out in public together. We were still a secret. Countess invitations to a dinner out were refused. A trip to the store was even off limits for the two of us.

I began to feel like I was living in a very small cage. I must admit though, the cage that held me was a gorgeous space. It was a confinement unlike any I could have imagined before meeting her.

I was well taken care of, but one day, boredom began to set in. I longed for the big city, the restaurants and shops, the hustle bustle, and the opportunity to study vast and varied characters, gaining material for a new book, as yet unwritten.

Considering my options, I asked her to leave Mussel Shoals and to come with me to Seattle. I assured her we could spend most of the time in Alabama. I explained my needs and my desire to go back to my new view condo, which I hadn't set foot inside of, in nearly five months.

I did not ask her to be my bride.

She declined my Seattle offer, saying she could not leave the Sunday school; that she lived for and was born to teach the children.

When I brought up the fact that there were many churches in Seattle, and that she could easily find a class to teach, she said it wouldn't be the same.

I was trapped between my desire to go back to the city of my birth, and the desires that she bridled so well and so often.

It was then that she began to change.

She had me hooked. It was evidenced in my inability to leave. She knew full well that I had a life, or a semblance of one elsewhere. However, I seemed powerless to just pack up the few possessions I had brought from my other life and to return to it.

It seemed she reveled in my weakness. Slowly, subtly, she began increasing her hold on me. Anytime I would bring up the subject of leaving, she would come to me for a few nights in a row. Those evenings that ran into the early morning hours were beyond description. I could have died a happy man on any of those wondrous occasions without regrets.

In darkness, she was primal. In daylight, she wore a conservative dress. When night fell, in the privacy of my rented home, with the curtains drawn, when she had walked through the woods and left her car at her home, she changed and would ravage me for hours.

I had thought before meeting Leilauna that my needs were nearly insatiable. I had chalked it up to a decade and a half of marriage nearly without sex and, certainly devoid of tenderness. She made up for those lost years with frenzy.

After a few nights in a row, where love, tenderness, and naked brazen sexuality left me weak in the knees, the drought would come.

She would refuse my advances and avoid my home. Our ritual of swimming at the spring was placed on hold by colder weather. She would be distant. So distant that it seemed I no longer knew this woman—a woman I had begun to think of as my very best friend.

In the quiet hours of my loneliness without her, I pondered.

I had finally made the decision. I packed my bags, closed up the house, and went to Leilauna's, intending to say goodbye for a few months.

I was tired of the secrecy and of the hidden relationship. I needed desperately to get away. I needed distance from her so that I could think rationally.

In her living room, I told her my plans and said my goodbyes.

She came to me in that way. I could not refuse, and she led me to her room. It was the first time we had been intimate in her home. She did things to me that day that I will not describe in print but leave you, the reader, to imagine.

It had been morning when I came to say goodbye. When at last she finally released me, the sun had been down for hours.

I staggered to my car, went back to my rented house, and fell into bed.

Chapter 20

WHEN I AWOKE, I smelled bacon frying. I could hear her in the kitchen singing a soft melody. In that moment, I weakened. I thought of the "M" word, and how wonderful it would be to wake up like this every morning.

The well-trained voice in my head screamed, "NO! DON'T DO IT, JAY!"

I came to my senses, shook my head from side to side to clear the haze that had me considering what I had long ago swore I would never do again. Then I got up and went into the kitchen.

The drapes were pulled, of course. She had on a little silk teddy that was bright red. I had never seen her wear that color before. She was absolutely radiant, in a slightly flashy way. I'd not seen her wear make-up before either. This morning she was. It was a little heavy, and was done very well. I was intrigued by the change.

We ate smiling and making very pleasant small talk. The way she ate her food was suggestive. In fact, even the way she had flipped the bacon and scrambled the eggs, seemed directed by her exuding sexuality. When she buttered the toast, I felt myself becoming aroused. *Down! NOW! Down!* I thought silently.

After breakfast, she coaxed me back to bed, saying she was tired and wanted to take a nap.

I had learned in the past two months to enjoy her company whenever she offered it. When she took my hand, I followed. I was like a chipmunk gathering nuts and storing them for a frigid winter. Soon there would be no food available for a time.

My accumulated stash of intimate interludes would have to see me though until spring. My metaphor might be weak, but that is how I related to a scenario that was becoming predictable and somewhat frightening.

The woman that I loved without reserve had me on a tether. It was made from a myriad of her wondrous talents: her beauty, work ethic, tenderness, love, sensuality…shall I go on?

I'm sure that by now you are getting the picture. All was not well in paradise.

When we woke, it was afternoon. The sun was out, and I asked if she would like to take a walk.

She didn't answer verbally, but I understood that walking outside was out of the question.

Leilauna had in mind another form of exercise. She sat astride me and worked her magic. In that moment, just before euphoria is gained, she spoke softly. "Jay, I love you so much! We could be like this every day and night. You wouldn't have to sleep alone for days at a time any more. We could be seen in public. You understand what would be best, and would make me ever so happy, don't you, darling? I'm so confused. Don't you love me, dearest?"

We both swore love as though it was our last breath. Indeed, when she finished with me, I struggled for a time, regaining mine.

And so my training proceeded. However, I was unaware that I was being trained. I am blonde. I like blonde jokes and tell a few that are dear to me just to show I have no aversion to making fun of myself. I am, however, not stupid. All the wondrous testing of our public school system ingrained that fact into me early on.

Naiveté is another thing entirely.

I like to think of myself as a trusting person. I like to believe in the inherent goodness of human kind. Do you get the picture? To balance out that weakness, the trusting nature, I have formed cynicism into a vintage label all my own.

Cynicism is my guardian. During my very drawn out divorce, I had honed it to a razor's edge. Unfortunately, when it came to Leilauna…I had none. She easily erased that discerning side of my nature when I was with her. Therefore, in retrospect, I realized she had deftly disarmed me.

I was unsure of her intent. To me, it didn't matter. She fed me and took care of my needs. She was, to me, a heaven on Earth. I had followed her, blinded by her passion and beauty and kindness and sexiness and work ethic…. Oh right! I have covered all these points before.

I was following her lead. Like a lamb to the slaughter.

I asked her to marry me. Can you believe that? Jay, with the iron heart…. Her furnace had heated the iron into a red hot mass that was about to burst into streaming rivulets of molten metal. I had to do something. It was the only thing that made sense. After a thousand hours of vacillating, I had decided my course.

I popped the question, ring in hand. I did, however, condition my very romantic proposal on a pre-nup.

She was ecstatic, and then heartbroken.

How could it be that I didn't trust her? Weren't we best friends? What if something happened to dear old Jay? How would she be able to survive financially? Wouldn't it be great to walk around in public with her on my arm, our heads held high, our values and morals beyond reproach among the narrow minded backwards southern religious blanket that was stifling my happiness and hers?

She asked a lot of questions. Looking into her big brown eyes, they all made sense.

Her questions were good, and I could answer most of them easily. Her arguments were persuasive, her looks endearing. All of it combined would not quell the nagging fear I had of marriage. Most of all, I remembered slaving like a dog for fifteen years in a failed marriage, only to see the lazy slob of a so-called housewife walk away with the lion's share of my sweat and blood, or as some people refer to it—money.

I loved Leilauna without reserve. Except the reserves that were under lock and key. I had no intention of giving that key away in the throes of passion.

My cynicism in check, I went to see John. I needed a beer and some good advice.

Chapter 21

BIG JOHN WAS not nearly as big as he had been when I came to Mussel Shoals. I was surprised.

"What's up, my man?" I asked, pretending I didn't notice that he must have lost fifty pounds in the past month and a half.

"Always the same around here; you know that, Jay. What's my favorite action hero up to today? You killin' any bad guys, or putting out devastating fires, or maybe helping a damsel in distress fix up a dilapidated old farm?" He winked conspiratorially.

"Funny…very funny." I could tell he was waiting to see if I noticed his weight loss. He had that look of anticipation in his eyes—the same kind of look you might see from a kid waiting in line to sit on Santa's lap.

I kept him in suspense and pretended I didn't notice. I needed him focused.

"I need a beer, John."

His look changed. That's one of the many things I like about John. His face is like a picture book of emotions. If *National Geographic* ever did a pictorial on the range of human emotions, Big John could easily be their poster child.

Right now, he wore a look of perplexity. I could tell he was concerned because the beer didn't come out real fast. It was still sleeping under that makeshift bar. I wanted it awakened. I needed its company.

"Problems ain't solved by the inside of a can, Jay. You back to drinking?"

"No."

"Then why you starting today? You know what an imbecile you can be when that stuff gets the better of you. What if *you know who* finds out?"

His words brought my senses, which were spiraling downward in a sea of despair, back up for air. I was in the real world again, not the make believe one where alcohol solves problems.

"Thanks, John." I noticed that the can was still under the bar. This big man really was my friend.

"So, what's up with the weight loss? I didn't know you were going in to have all that blubber surgically removed." It was my turn to be playful. This game entertained us. Otherwise, John's place might be found in Webster's as one of the many definitions for boredom.

"For your information, *smart ass*, the wife and I changed our diets. The doctor been sayin' we need to drop the excess, so we working on it."

He smiled. "You know I grew up eating fried chicken, country fried steak, biscuits and gravy, and all that scrumptious deep fried seafood. Back then, my body processed that stuff like an industrial garbage disposal. But the last… well, I don't want to think about the years…that type of food hasn't been agreeing with me.

"The wife got a book on food combinations, and we been eating a lot more healthy. I been drinking a lot of pure spring water, too. And the biggest thing is the cayenne pepper. It is burning the blubber, as you so graciously put it, right off our old bodies. Doctor says my heart is getting stronger, too—that's because of the cayenne."

He laughed. "Hell, my sex drive's even coming back. That old girl of mine is lookin' pretty damn hot in that new bod of hers—mmm...mmm...mmm. I do declare, she was hell for looks when I met her!"

"John, I'm happy for you, but you and your wife...and sex...could you please? I don't need that picture in my overactive imagination. As for turning over a new leaf when it comes to your health, that's awesome!" I high-fived him and said, "You look great, man! I didn't know that underneath all that lard there was a good looking old man!"

"Old man gonna kick your butt if you're not careful," he said. "How would you like that?"

"John! Come on, man, I was just joking!"

"So was I, moron."

We laughed together, and my craving for my old liquid friend passed.

John quit rumbling and got serious. "What's new with you, Jay? What you doing that makes you want the can again?"

"It's her."

"You want to spill?"

"You think I came down here for your company? I can't afford a shrink.... Besides, the advice you've given me has been on the mark. I need some more."

"Fool gonna listen this time? Or fool gonna go off with that big know-it-all head, and his dick leading him around like a little dog on a leash?"

"Have I been that bad?"

"Don't know. You ain't been coming to see Big John much. She been locking you in a closet or something?"

I had never thought of my relationship with Leilauna in that new light. The sun rose on the idea, and I took in the possibilities.

I said, quietly, sheepishly, "Kind of, I guess."

"Fool got it bad. Huh?"

He started laughing again, only this time I wasn't laughing with him. I was thinking. Flashes of realization passed through my mind. It was like a brilliant strobe light was illuminating all the most strategic scenes between her and me. It was a trip that made me smile and excited me at the same time.

"Where did you go, boy?"

John's big voice brought me in from la-la land, and I re-entered my body, or so it seemed. There he was looking at me with that parental seriousness. He wanted answers. I was ready to give them.

I was thankful it was early; his six loyal customers had not yet finished their morning bowls of cream of wheat.

"I asked her to marry me, John."

"And?" See, there was that shrink technique again.

"She said she wouldn't do it. Not with a pre-nup anyway."

"A pre-nup? That was part of your proposal? Classy, romantic, *and* sensitive. You idiot! That's not how you do it! You woo her, and let her get used to the idea for a while, then you start getting down to the nitty-gritty stuff. You dumber than I thought!"

"I know, John. I just can't seem to get it right with her. I can't live without her though."

"Drummer boy got it bad! That's your dick controlling your brain again. Is she really *that* good?"

"I'm sworn to secrecy."

"Oh! Man, I ain't askin' for details. I just want to know how deep the water is, and how far from shore you've drifted while you've been blinded by her...shall I say *charisma,* for lack of a more gentle word?"

"It's deep, John, and I can't see the shoreline anymore. The worst part is that even though the water is warm, tender, refreshing, and inviting—and seems like paradise most of the time—I keep getting this niggling feeling that a hungry pack of tiger sharks is nearby, just waiting to get a scent of me. Then paradise instantly becomes a bloodbath. My blood! You know what I mean?"

"I met a woman like that once. She was really something, but she was a hardened city girl. I decided on marrying the country type. Maybe not quite so exciting, but safer ground. I don't enjoy swimming in shark infested waters—it takes the relaxation away."

"I know, John. That is why I'm so serious about Leilauna. I like her old fashioned values and the fact that she was sheltered growing up here."

John's big eyes got wide. He had that deer in the headlights look.

Concerned, I said, "What?"

"You don't know?"

"Know what?"

"She's not *from* here. She didn't grow up here, Jay!"

"What are you talking about? She grew up on her grandmother's farm!"

"Is that what she told you?"

I thought hard. I thought about all the conversations that had passed between Leilauna and me. I thought about all the things she had said about her childhood and realized frantically, that I really didn't know anything tangible about her upbringing.

"Well, not exactly," I answered.

"What did she tell you?"

"Not much. I guess she just spoke of her love for her grandmother and the farm and how it was a shame so many country folk don't take more pride in maintaining their ancestral homes and barns."

"And from that scant info you just *assumed* she was from here?"

He emphasized the word, ass-umed, and I remembered the old adage painfully.

He was shaking that big head again. This time, the big neck inner tubes were gone. I liked that…that they were gone. They had been a little disconcerting.

I had worried once or twice that as large as John was, and as old as he was, that a turn of misfortune would take him from me before his wisdom and intrinsic healing powers had fixed me.

"Yes, I guess I assumed."

That southern silence took over. Within it, I became more uncomfortable.

John was obviously allowing me time to adjust to the new and intellectually slamming info, that Leilauna might *not* be the sheltered, old-fashioned southern type I had believed she was when I had begun my marathon race to win her over.

"Do you want to know what I know? It ain't much."

"Yes, please," I said, nodding vigorously. "Enlighten me."

John got serious. He could do that, but it was rare.

"Well, I know that her mother grew up here, on the farm you've been slaving away on." He gave me a wry wink just to add a little levity at a critical time. My mind was reeling.

He continued. "That is, at least until she ran away when she was sixteen with one of those rock bands that used to record here. It seems her mother loved the flashy, long-haired types that rolled in and out of Mussel Shoals in them days.

"I know her mother had the child out of wedlock, and it was quite a scandal down here. When I came back from the war in seventy-two, everyone was talking about it." He shook his head. "Anyway, her mother bounced around for years. She had the young girl with her most the time, but would drop her at her gram's anytime she had something hot going on with one of them band members.

"I guess you would call her a groupie. We learned that term down here in the seventies. It was a very bad word, a word that shocked tradition.

"There were a lot of local girls who succumbed to the pull of the life of travel, free love, endless drugs, and an opportunity to believe they were really someone important, when all the while they were just shadows in the background of the stars. They were passed around and changed out like soiled underwear. Most of them ended up back here, burned out and looking old before their time.

"Leilauna's mother never came back. Well, I mean to stay. She always looked good, too! It was like she had self-control and was searching for her mark in life. She never showed up here like so many of the others, aged and lifeless from running flat out chasing a futile dream, a dream that left them dirty and washed out, with nothing but painful memories in the end. No," he said, shaking his head, "that one was definitely different.

"She would show up here with the girl, and visit the old woman for a day or two before dropping the child off for a spell. She was always driving the best of cars and dressed in the latest flash.

"Many of the gossipers down here labeled her a woman of the evening, or worse. How else could she have achieved that affluence in so little time? they said. Anyway no one has seen her here for...I don't know, maybe eight years. That was the last time. Leilauna would have been near full grown, maybe sixteen at the time.

"People here speculate that her mother died or that the two of them had a falling out of sorts. The girl arrived on a bus, dressed in simple clothes, and was traveling with one suitcase. She always fit in here, and she was no different then.

"She was older. Just the prettiest little thing you could imagine. Of course she had always been a head turner, that one. Lots of people speculate down here on who her father is. Truth be known…no one knows.

"She settled in here and started going to church right off. She played forward on the basketball team, finished high school with honors, and helped her grandma run the farm. She stayed away from boys, even though three counties worth were trying desperately to win her affections. She's always been a quiet one, sticking to herself and not socializing much.

"I always figured she was that way to keep the local gossips from learning anything juicy about her past, or her mother's. I guess that's about it, Jay. Hope the info helps."

"I have just learned more about the woman of my dreams from you than I have from her in nearly five months!"

"What you going to do?"

"I don't know, John…I honestly don't know."

"Jay…I'm going to live dangerously. I'm going to give you some advice. I won't be held responsible for what happens, if you choose to follow it. You are a big boy. You are responsible for your own life."

"Sounds fair, lay it on me."

"When you arrived in Mussel Shoals, you were a wreck. Now I know you got your success. You got money and the prestige a successful writer achieves. But still, I saw you for what you were back then—a pitiful shame."

"Be serious!" I said, shocked at his evaluation of who I was upon arriving in Mussel Shoals. I wanted an explanation.

"I *am* being serious, Jay, serious as a heart attack. Listen to me, will you? This is important!"

I opened my ears and my mind to the big man. I became a proverbial sponge soaking up all the wisdom he graciously imparted.

Most of it shocked me in the beginning.

In the end, I was almost in tears. He had struck a chord in me that had not been strummed in decades. I saw everything clearly and don't believe I ever would have without his native intelligence and common sense.

When he finished, I jumped up, ran around the bar, and gave him a bear hug. I was baby bear; he was papa bear. It felt good to me.

He allowed it for the briefest moment, then said, "Sit down, fool! What people goin' to think if they see you and me like this?"

Here is what he imparted, or as close as I can remember.

"You was a mess, Jay. Whenever someone feels that alcohol deserves the lion's share of their time, they living, but they ain't livin' life. They existing until the day *that* shit consumes them.

"They most often end up alone, disheveled, and talking to themselves, because they've lost all the people in their life that were important, because the alcohol took precedence.

"I've seen it too many times. Most of the guys, my buddies from 'Nam that made it back home succumbed. Ain't many of them left. They all went down the road I just laid out for you.

"You, Jay, were a long way down that road. I thought it the moment I laid eyes on you. When you sucked five beers down in an hour, I knew it for sure."

"Since coming here, you've changed, Jay. Whatever you do, don't go back to the can. If you did, you will rob yourself of everything meaningful that is in your future. Oh, I'm not saying never have a beer again. I'm just saying don't use it as a crutch. Don't drink 'cause you're stressed, or sad, or perturbed. That's where problem drinking begins. You got to deal with problems sober and clear headed, not in some haze of alcohol-induced confidence. That confidence is an illusion; it will always let you down hard.

"Anyway, here is my take on Leilauna: She changed you. For her, you became a better person. You finished your book, you took on a trade, even if it was a ploy to get in her pants, it worked, and so you achieved the success many sober men would only dream of.

"Now you're sitting here feeling sorry for yourself because you want this woman for your wife...which is a devastating realization because she won't marry you with a pre-nup! I don't have any sympathy for you. You don't marry her and you gonna regret it! I told you I have a sixth sense about these things, and it's screaming at me now!"

"I can't, John," I said.

"Can't what?"

"Marry her without a pre-nup."

"Why not, Jay?" John looked tired. He really couldn't be because it was early afternoon. I realized he was showing tiredness on his face because he was dealing with my mental gymnastics.

"Simply because I swore off marriage," I said. "Now I *am* considering it, which is a major hurdle for me to get over, and I can't make the leap without a pre-nup!"

John just shook his head and then started in with that frustrating reasoning he was so fond of.

"Look Jay, she makes you happy, right?"

"Happy is too weak a word."

"You love her, right?"

"I would gladly sacrifice myself to a gruesome and painful death, protecting her. That is MY definition of love, so yes!"

"You two are sexually compatible?"

"Two peas in a pod!"

"And you work well together?"

"Like a family of beavers felling timber and constructing a dam!"

"You were lonely and not very happy before you met her, right?"

Now this was a tough one. It took some deep introspection. I spent about five seconds digging through the bowels of my psyche before answering. "Yes, John…I guess I was unhappy and didn't realize it. There are so many levels of happiness and unhappiness that sometimes the two get confused.

"I thought I was so *so* happy when my divorce was final. Now looking back on it, assisted by your ever brutal insight, I realize that I was not really happy…I just was a whole lot less miserable. So that mental state passed for happiness. Does that make any sense?"

John nodded but kept quiet, so I kept talking.

"I arrive here in Mussel Shoals. I am a somewhat successful and a critically recognized author. I think I'm happy, but again…it was an illusion because I was less *down* than when I was climbing the nearly insurmountable mountain of a published literary career.

"I had successfully scaled a treacherous peak that eats aspiring writers by the millions. I thought I was on top of the world. But I had no idea what the top of the world felt like. So again, I was mistaken."

I sighed. "Then I meet the woman of my dreams. She is tastefully younger than myself…."

John's eyebrows raised.

I continued, unruffled, "She fulfills me. I am happy constantly when I'm with her. She's honest, sincere, hard-working, and most of all, she is the most thoughtful woman I have ever been with. She is perfect for me."

"And?" he asked, as if he really already knew the answer.

"And I'm in a stalemate. I'm playing a life-threatening game. On one side of the board is my financial security and my oath against marriage. There is also questionable and desperately illusive happiness. The other side of the board is…is…."

"Yes, Jay?"

"Is Leilauna, a veritable treasure trove of happiness and fulfillment. Why, the woman herself could be the guardian Goddess at the gates of ancient Xanadu!"

"Then why are you sitting here? Why don't you go and sweep her away in wedded bliss?"

"The sharks, John…."

"Shit, man, I tell you what I think. I was hoping you could come to the realization on your own, but your denseness surprises me constantly.

"You marry her. Worst case scenario? It don't work out. What you get is *her* in your bed every night for the duration. You get her on your arm in public…I can see that ego of yours bloating up right now, your head gets bigger because people envy the man who married Leilauna!

"So you experience wedded bliss for a time, and then it turns sour…let's just take ole Murphy into the equation. She divorces you and takes half of everything you own. You have still experienced true happiness for as long as it lasts.

"Do you know how many men I know that would gladly give everything they own to be with her? And here you are sniveling about potentially having to give her half? Man, you're denser than I thought!

"You can always write another book, and make more money. You think you going to find another one out there like Leilauna? If you do, you're kidding yourself!"

I was about talked out and had absorbed just about all the new info I could handle. At the same time, the author in me saw another angle on the Mussel Shoals story. I mean, I thought I was finished with the book…but what if I included the heart rending of families seeing their beloved young daughters run off as groupies, only to be used, abused, and discarded. Then the girls returning home, burned out and used up.

I had to admit that while the piece I had written had a lot of history, it lacked the human interest side that could truly make it Pulitzer material…perhaps I ought to stay awhile longer and work that side of the story, I thought.

"Hey John, thanks for allowing me to cry on your shoulder and for the advice. I'm going to think about everything you've said real hard."

"Why is it, Jay…that I don't feel your sincerity?"

"Could be that new diet of yours. It might be messing with that big antennae you're so proud of."

"Get out of here! But don't come whining to me if you disregard my advice and end up miserable!" He smiled. That meant he was kidding…sort of.

Chapter 22

I WASN'T IN the mood to work, nor was I in a writer's frame of mind. I just needed some time to cool, and to think.

I thought about the dock at the old mill. I was interested in fishing. If I did stay a while longer, it might be a good way to pass the time. I might even get some new info on the storyline I was thinking of following. I hadn't sent the book off for editing yet. There was still plenty of time to add some content. I decided on going down to the dock, to see if any of the locals were wetting a line.

This time the potholes on the old mill road were no problem. The old panel wagon had plenty of clearance. As I neared the structures, there were two pick-up trucks parked, and it looked like four guys in the shade of the old army tarp, out on the dock.

I parked out of the way and walked out towards the men in the shade.

Ben was the first one to greet me. I recognized one of the others from the day I had bought Ben's truck.

"How's that old Ford working out, Jay?"

"Honestly, very good. I haven't had a bit of trouble with her or the tools. I appreciate how well you took care of everything."

"Jay…I've always been one for the details. I'm a stitch-in-time kind of guy. What are you doing down here this fine day?"

"I thought maybe I could learn a little about fishing. I may be staying awhile longer. I haven't quite finished my story, and need a little more time."

"Be happy to teach you. First thing a man needs fishing for gar is patience."

"I had a wife once that taught me that art." I smiled knowingly, and the four men chuckled, understanding the humor immediately."

Ben asked, "You divorced then?"

"Yeah…for about five years now."

"Must've been tough going through something like that."

"Going through it was no picnic, but afterward I felt just like I'd been released from doing fifteen years of hard prison time."

They all laughed again. I was settling right in and being accepted.

I was looking at the water again. It struck me how it wasn't muddy like all the other water in the rivers I'd seen around here.

"Sometime when you guys aren't fishing, I'd like to come down and see if I could swim across the river and back. I used to be a distance swimmer in college."

Ben looked away from me and at the others for a moment. Two of the men had wry humor showing on their faces; the other was deadpan.

Ben looked back to me and said, with a very serious look, "Swimmin' in this river would be a very bad idea."

"Why's that, Ben?"

"The Alligator Gar, some of them be big as a house. People disappear when they start swimming here."

I had never heard of an Alligator Gar. I thought he might be pulling my leg. So I asked an intelligent question. "Just how big *is*, as big as a house, Ben?"

I had seen some pretty small houses down here. Most people would call them shacks, but the locals referred to them as houses. So my curiosity was up.

He looked pretty serious and said, "You watch that float with the green stripe on it. Green's my official color. You watch, and if it starts rolling out line, you holler. I'll be right back."

"Where you going, Ben?"

"To get my photo book. You wouldn't believe me, lest I show you."

I looked at the other three, and they just sat there straight faced, nodding in agreement.

Nothing exciting happened with the line, and I had watched it without blinking. I don't know how fast these critters were, but I didn't want to lose one on my watch.

Ben came back with a well-worn leather bound picture album. He opened it up, and inside there were pictures of fish that a person could only imagine in their worst nightmares. First of all, they were huge. They were shown hanging on a scale, and I saw weights that went up to four hundred pounds and more. The freakiest part was they had a long snout, much like an alligator, and the snouts all bristled with nasty looking teeth.

I wasn't a greenhorn and knew this must be a trick photo book...you know, like the postcards with a trout the size of a horse in the back of a pick-up truck.

I said, "Come on, you guys, there really can't be fish like this out there." I pointed out to the placid blue water. No one laughed. They were acting very serious—at least I believed they were acting.

One of the others spoke up. "They ain't out there now, could be any time though."

"What do you mean they aren't out there now? If they aren't out there, then what are you guys doing fishing for them?"

"The color of the water changes when they come. They stir up the bottom with their massive tails. The water gets murkier, and this helps them hunt their prey. They roam in packs like wolves and share their kill. They've been known to devour a full grown steer, bones and all, faster than you can tie your shoes."

"You guys are playing me, right?" I asked. "Fish that eat cows, running in packs...why haven't I ever heard of these fish before?"

"You familiar with *all* the fish of the Amazon?"

"Course not. What does the Amazon have to do with *this* river system?"

"Let me explain it to him." It was Ben again, the others nodded quietly, backing up his story as it unfolded? I was beginning to be a believer. When he was finished, I was convinced.

"You see, Jay, some years back, the government banned the hunting of alligators. They said the reptile in the Mississippi and other southern rivers were nearing extinction. Course at the time, no one believed it.

"The hunting stopped. Poachers were heavily fined, their guns and trucks confiscated. Years went by, and the population of them critters exploded. With nobody hunting, they started showing up in folk's back yards. Some toddlers disappeared, and there were tracks—tracks that led right to the water."

"We all knew what was happening. But the government threw millions at the problem and studied it for years. Nothing was done to diminish the ever-burgeoning population of the creatures, and the problems escalated.

"The US government that had banned the hunting was staring some major liability lawsuits in the face. You see, by taking away our rights to hunt them and to protect our children and our livestock, the government became the one to sue. Claims were quickly and silently paid off and settled out of court. Many of them were bogus stock claims, and some crafty dirt poor farmers cashed in.

"The monumental size of the problem was covered up by the federal government. There were also missing children, and I'm not talking a few. The government blamed it on serial killers. But when a child disappears from a back yard, and a fence is mangled in the process and the tracks and blood lead into the water, it's pretty lame to blame some wacko.

"Meanwhile the problem got worse, and all that the bonehead biologists did was collect fat checks and retirement accounts. They did nothing to curb the problem. Then some enterprising person from the private sector realized that the Amazon had few problems like we did, even though their native reptile species were not being heavily hunted by man. The reason: The Amazonian Alligator Gar. You see, the Gar eat the young alligators. They are the only known predatory fish that go after the gators.

"So this enterprising fellow, who will remain anonymous, imported some of the fish, and now the gator and croc population is under control. Of course, now we have a serious monster of a game fish, and few problems with reptiles in our back yards."

"How long ago were these Gar imported from South America?" I asked, astounded.

"No way to be certain, but people started catching a few about thirty years back." Ben looked like he was finished.

I looked back out over the seemingly peaceful river with a new respect for lurking monster fish, which could darken its door any minute.

We sat in silence for a while and thought.

After a time, I spoke up. "You guys probably know I'm writing a piece on Mussel Shoals and the way the southern band boom affected the town." It was no secret. I had been asking a lot of different people a series of mundane questions.

They all nodded.

"I want to include in the story something more from a human interest perspective, and wondered if you guys know anyone who had daughters run away...you know, and follow the bands."

It was like I had dropped a big icicle in someone's fresh hot cup of coffee. I got some looks that were unreadable but didn't look too friendly or open. One of the men, who I had no name for, spoke softly, reverently, like he was attending a funeral.

"Some folk carryin' a lot of grief...might be a topic they won't want written about."

No one added a thing. I looked at Ben, and he was gazing out across the water. To me...it didn't seem like he was watching anything in particular. His eyes seemed a bit glassy and unfocused.

The day's mood had unexplainably shifted. I really had no idea at the time why it had. I can be dense and unfeeling. Just ask John. But I felt it like storm clouds obscuring the sun on an otherwise beautiful day. I felt the cool and decided to take my leave.

"Thanks for telling me about the Gar and letting me sit with you guys," I said. "I hope you don't mind if I come back some time?"

Ben looked to me as I stood up. His eyes were soft. They had a quality I hadn't seen in them before. I couldn't place my finger on it, but there was something.

He said, "You come on down anytime, Jay. We be happy for your company…maybe you'll bring us some good luck."

Chapter 23

I DROVE UP the river road thinking about my talk on the dock, and with John. My mind was spinning with information. I drove by Leilauna's farm, and to my own. I needed some down time to consider the things I had learned.

Could Leilauna be less than the wholesome, sheltered southern girl I had fallen in love with?

I am the first to admit to my naiveté, but could I have been that blind as well? Some of the techniques she practiced while we were making love had surprised me. I just figured the act to be so primal in nature that she was working on genetic memory or something. I had no reason to believe she had any experience in those things. Yet if she had not grown up sheltered by the church here, then where had she been? And what kind of things had she been doing?

You see why I needed some think time?

The red silk teddy and the well-done heavy make-up should have been a clue. I just thought she had bought a copy of *Vogue* or something. Women do that, don't they? Buy a magazine and practice applying make-up like the magazine's pictures show? Could it be explained so simply?

After thinking for a while, I realized I didn't care about Leilauna's background or where she had been before moving to Mussel Shoals permanently. Everyone had a skeleton or two in their closet. I just hoped that she didn't have too many.

I went to bed and couldn't sleep. I decided to get up and get some work done outlining the topic of southern bands and runaway groupies. I thought that in the absence of actual fact, I could at least construct an outline and work on where the new material would weave into what I had already written.

It was about 1 am when I heard a key in the front door dead bolt. She was here! My heart raced, and I forgot all my doubts. The trepidation left me like a fifty does when you fill your gas tank. It was that easy.

I turned from my computer to greet her. What I saw would have frightened me if I hadn't known it was Leilauna. She had on black lipstick, and her hair was pulled up in one of those vertical pony tails, or whatever they are called. Her hair looked like a horn protruding from the top of her head. It was adorned with various wooden, silver, and golden bracelets that were very striking. The rest of her make-up was...I guess you would say gothic: dark, thick eyeliner, and eye shadow with little sequins. She reminded me of a vampiress I had seen in a sexy, scary movie.

I had often fantasized about what I would do if ever I were making love to a vampire woman and at that critical moment, when the victim is entering ecstasy and the blood-starved hussy goes for the jugular with those wicked teeth—

I could never say that I would definitely have the willpower to shut-off an orgasm and save myself by saying no, I didn't want to give blood, and then going home unsatisfied.

See that's where the vampiress always get her man. So many of us are so pitifully desperate for affection, we would gladly suffer an eternity as one of the walking dead, just for an extremely satisfactory orgasm.

She didn't say a word, just grabbed me by the front of my flannel pajamas and shoved me towards the bed. I could have resisted, but what would the point be?

I desperately wanted what she was willing to dish out. She was so different. I had never seen *that* forceful side of her.

I have always had a penchant for strong women. In the past, some of my choices got me in a little deeper than I had anticipated. Tonight I was with my best friend and lover. I trusted Leilauna. I was relaxed. My anticipation made it all the better.

A couple hours later, when we were on the edge and ready to break over—in that moment when every man is at his weakest—she whispered, "I can be anything you want, Jay."

I truly believed she could. I said, "Please, bite my neck!"

Chapter 24

MORNING CAME AS it did sometimes, with her cooking and me waking up with a steaming mug of coffee beside the bed. I rubbed my eyes and thought about the evening past, with a longing in my lower half, as I went into the kitchen.

She was wearing a conservative white dress. It was the one with the floral pattern she had been wearing that day so long ago, when we had met for the first time. She had removed the make-up and her hair was down, lying softly beneath her shoulders.

I hugged her from behind and said softly, "Thanks for coming over." She rubbed into me in a not-so conservative way, and my mind flew into that heavenly place only she possessed. What this woman could do with a glance or a gentle touch was magic.

She broke away lightly and served.

The breakfast was done well: scrambled eggs with smoked ham, whole grain toast with real butter, and some strawberry jam she had made herself. I bucked up on the coffee. It was black and hot and went down *just* so nicely. All the while, we ate in silence. She would look at me the way she always did at breakfast, exuding sweetness, smiles, and sunshine. I said silently to myself, *Jay, you are a lucky man.*

"What are you up to today, honey-cake?"

She called me that rarely. I melted when she did. "Anything you would like," I answered. I was the definition of agreeable. I waited to hear her next words.

"Well…it's midweek…I don't have school 'til Sunday. I was wondering if you might like to drive down to the Gulf. We could rent one of those romantic oceanfront rooms and make uninterrupted love for the next three days."

"Let me check my schedule. All clear! When would you like to leave? I could be ready in three minutes!"

"Oh, Jay, we'll have to leave this evening, when it's dark. That way none of the local gossips will see us together. Is that okay with you?"

"Sure!"

"Pick me up at seven then. We can drive the bug. No sense in taking your tool truck, is there?"

"No, the VW is a much better choice."

With that, we cleaned up the breakfast mess together, and she disappeared into the woods behind the house.

When she was out of sight, I did the dance of joy! We would drive down tonight and wouldn't have to drive back until Saturday evening. Oh MY! Three and a half days with her, and with no pruded-up, busy body gossipmongers to worry about. We could walk the beaches, take in the sights, wine and dine at upper crust eateries. I was ecstatic.

The day drug on. I couldn't focus on my writing. Instead, I took a long walk and sprinted a bit to get my wind up. I found myself whistling again. I was amazed by that.

Chapter 25

COMPARED TO MUSSEL Shoals, the ocean at the Gulf was another planet entirely.

We could be ourselves—uninhibited, carefree, and openly in love. It was wonderful, and I found myself wanting to be with her like this, always.

We swam and walked the beaches. We did the tourist tour of the little shops. We held and kissed in public. I was living the life I had dreamed of a thousand times. I was here with her, and she with me, without the hiding.

The protesting voice in my head kept speaking. It had been talking so much these past couple of months that it had grown hoarse from overuse. I could hardly hear it anymore.

My optimistic side was winning. Leilauna *looked* like my wife. As we walked along arm in arm, the heads of men young and old craned to take in her flowing beauty.

John had been right. It all made my head swell just a little.

The time flew like water dashing over a falls. The three days were gone before I knew it. I had had her for seventy-two hours non-stop, but it was time to go back to the little town where we would have to hide our true feelings and live life as a sham.

We didn't say too much that was notable on the drive back. We were both worn out. We had spent more time in the sack than we had out of doors. It now seemed a fiction. Now I had to wake up.

Finally, in the last hour of the drive, with her asleep leaning on my shoulder, I said, "Leilauna, darling?" She awakened and looked to me with the tired, innocent eyes of a child.

"Please come with me to Seattle. It will be like the past three days always. No more hiding...no more worrying about being seen together. You said you'd like to see Seattle—come with me. I have to go before too long. I haven't been home in over six months."

She didn't even consider it. Without any time for contemplation, she said, "No."

We drove the rest of the way to Mussel Shoals in silence.

Rolling up Leilauna's driveway, I was reminiscing about the past few days. It hit me when I saw her house. We had been living a fantasy. I wanted to continue it. Her answer of "no" had brought my blood up a bit. I was feeling pushed, and I felt like pushing back.

I helped her with her two bags, kissed her lightly, and said, "You are wonderful. Thanks for the get-away." We said goodnight pleasantly, and I kissed her one last time before leaving for the evening.

On the short hop home, I decided that I needed some time away from Leilauna and from Mussel Shoals. The problem was the book. I had to stay. I was eager to begin the new writing.

Chapter 26

THERE WAS A knock on the door that jarred me awake. I squinted and looked out of the bedroom window. The sun appeared to be high in the sky, and the day was bright.

I put my slippers on and went to the door.

I was pleasantly surprised to see that it was Ben. I opened the door and greeted him. "Hey Ben, what's up? I was working late last night, so you caught me still in bed."

"I'd be happy to come back another time…if that's better."

"No! Just come on in! I don't get many visitors, so you surprised me. Have a seat. I'll throw some clothes on. I feel a little odd entertaining in my pjs."

I directed him to the living room, rushed into my room, and tossed on some jeans and a t-shirt. I took a look in the dresser mirror and noticed that I had a big tuft of matted hair sticking up on the back of my head. I scraped a brush quickly through it and called it good.

Once I was back with Ben, I didn't start talking, he did. I was relieved, because I didn't know where to start.

"Jay, the reason I came up here was that I have a daughter. She was born out of wedlock. She left here with one of those bands, and she's never been back to see me. Oh, I heard she was in town a couple times, but I didn't know she was coming, and it wasn't to see me. I guess she's been embarrassed of her father."

"Why would she be embarrassed of you?" I asked.

"Because, I'm black."

I was taken aback. I wasn't expecting a twist, just a simple she left and didn't come back kind of story.

"I may be a little dense here…you're saying her mother is white?"

"Was."

"And the two of you weren't married?"

"No."

"Where is your daughter now, and how long has it been since you've seen her?"

"Near thirty years. I don't know where she is." He paused. "Jay…I don't mean to be pushy, but could I just tell you the story?"

"Absolutely. Do you mind if I take some notes?"

"I want you to do this right, Jay. I want your word that I can read what you write. If it's not just so, you and I will sit down together, and finish making it right. Okay?"

"You've got it," I said. "My word that you can edit it with me."

"Sounds fair then."

Ben had been sitting forward with hands on his knees. Leaning back in the chair, his eyes drifting out through the window, I could feel and see that his mind was rolling back the years.

"We grew up as children together…in the same part of town, I mean. I would see her on the walk to school sometimes, and would catch up and talk to her, while I was walking on the opposite side of the street.

"Black boys weren't allowed to walk with a white girl to school. That's how our friendship started, finding grey areas between the rules.

"She was a tomboy, that one. She had to wear a dress to school, but as soon as she was home, the dress came flying off. She'd be in her long pants or shorts, and we'd meet in the woods where no one was around.

"Sometimes we'd fish the hidden parts of creeks and swim in the deeper pools. We'd walk the woods talking and worked on building a fort way up in a big old live oak tree.

"We never did anything but what two boys would do. Except.... She talked real nice and proper and taught me to pronounce all the syllables and not to ever mumble." He stopped and laughed lightly, reminiscing a moment.

"She was *some* kind a stubborn, too. Well, when we started into our teens, everything changed. She was sent to a finishing school because they were trying to lady her up, and she wasn't cooperating.

"I would see her in the summers sometimes, and she would be polite and talk with me, but we never were the same kind of friends.

"She got married, and I'd see her now and then. We didn't talk those times, just said a polite hello and such. Then the war began, and we were sent away. When it was over, I came home. I understood that her husband had been killed in the taking of Iwo Jima.

"I bought a panel truck and started my handyman thing, and the years went by. I got married, had some kids, and bought a little house. Things were good. I was keeping busy and getting a lot of referral business because I was fair in my prices and dependable.

"Then one day I got referred by an old customer to someone new. They handed me a folded piece of paper, and I stuck it in my shirt pocket, thinking I would look at it later. That paper wasn't going to wait though. Soon as I put it in my pocket, I felt a kinda tingle, and I knew I was being told to look at it.

"I was driving along and I unfolded it. I stopped right then and turned around. I went to the new customer's house...you see, Jay, it was her...let's just call her...Molly... for now.

"Molly was living with her mother on the family farm. Two women—one getting on in years—and they needed some help with the place. It was quite a bit of acreage. There was always some fence mending to do, or carpentry and such. Molly would come and help sometimes, and we struck up our old friendship, just like we'd never been apart.

"She never remarried. I worked for her and the mother for some years keeping up the place, and one day, Molly's mother left this world, and Molly was alone.

"I would check in on her all the time, even if there was no work. We would visit and have a little lunch on the porch. Sometimes I would bring the food, other times, she would feed me.

"I guess...she was lonely...I never understood what happened really...my wife and I were happy. She *was* beautiful though, and I felt her sadness. Being on that big farm, alone with no family, she'd get a little melancholy sometimes. I guess once in a while, she just needed to be loved.

"I encouraged her to re-marry many times...but she never did.

"And so, Jay, that's how my daughter was born. I told you Molly was stubborn. When I realized she was pregnant, I offered to her get a real good doctor up north. I was concerned for her...you know, a baby out of wedlock in them days was a scandal. Also me being black and her white, that made it worse. I didn't want her ground through the grist mill of local gossip....

"She refused...to...have an abortion. She had decided to have a child. When she decided on getting something...

it was best not to be in her way...that's just the way it was going to be.

"She had red hair...I don't know if I told you that part. Molly didn't care what people thought. That was for sure.

"Anyway, she had...well, *we* had an angel...a little girl. She came and Molly was never happier. She wasn't alone anymore. I saw the little one all the time. Molly never told the child I was her father. I was just ole Ben the handyman.

"Well, it wasn't too surprising that our little girl would be stubborn, and oh *was* she. I can be that way myself sometimes. She was smart as a whip. And her skin wasn't dark at all. My family has some white blood, and I guess she drew those genes along with Molly's.

"Molly named her Azurelei. It was a strange name for down here in the south, but who was I to say? I started calling her Zurie for short, and it stuck.

"We had sixteen heavenly years, the three of us. When Zuri turned sixteen though, she became pretty much her own boss. Molly treated her like she was grown, and that might have been a mistake, but who can say in these things.

"Zurie loved music.... When the bands started coming...well, that's when it all changed, for the worse...then she was gone.

"Molly took it hard. She was never the same woman. She aged very rapidly and became an old woman before my eyes...it made my heart sick...but I didn't love her any less.

"You see, Jay...Zurie was Molly's daughter, but she was also her best friend. When she ran away, Molly took it like she had died or something. I believe, in the end, Molly succumbed to grief."

Ben's eyes were red and the last sentences came slower, with broken silent spaces draped between the words.

"Thanks, Ben...I'm glad you came this morning," I told him. "I was going to spend some time writing today...I will work on this. Come over tomorrow, and I'll have it printed and we can go over it. We will want to give it more body...those places...we can fill in together, okay?"

"Sure am obliged, Jay. Thank you."

He looked at me, and his eyes showed the wounding...the hurt. Then he spoke very softly. "I wish I could see her...Zurie, I mean. We were so close...when she was little...when she left...I cried, me and Molly both. We had lost our baby, and we just sobbed in each other's arms.

"My life's been through some bad days, Jay. That day though...was...the worst."

He paused, as if an emotional mental fog was clearing, and he was coming up through the years gone by, to the present. I waited silently. I didn't want to disrupt his thoughts.

"I talked with a few other people...folks that have stories to tell. Some have happy endings...others...well, you know everybody makes choices in life. Some don't work out too good. They want to talk with you, Jay. Folks in town...they feel it's time.

"If you want, I have their names and numbers written down. You can have the list if you're interested in speaking with them."

I nodded. "I would appreciate that, Ben. Going fishing today?" I asked him.

He shook his head. "Not today...I just don't feel like fishing right now. I'll see you tomorrow."

He walked out and got in his truck. As Ben left me, I was seeing this town in a very different light.

Chapter 27

Leilauna seemed to be in one of her famine cycles. I had been attempting to figure out exactly why she was so wonderful and loving for periods of time and then distantly removed in others. The cycles varied.

Sometimes it was a couple of weeks of bliss, and then two of loneliness for me. I thought the moon might be affecting her moods, and had marked a private calendar with the roller coaster of emotions she was forcing me to live. There was no pattern that I could see clearly.

I set my mind to some serious writing in what I had come to think of as the frozen wasteland of her "low love cycle."

I was beginning to think that she might be trying to manipulate me into something.... If she was...she had done a pretty good job. I had *almost* walked the plank off into those shark-infested waters.

All that in mind, I had decided to step back, and not act like a wild hyena starving for the tender morsels she so deftly controlled. I would play *this* cycle, like Cool Hand Luke.

I worked most of the day on Ben and Molly's story, except for a long walk to stretch out the kinks. The notes I had made turned into a touching and heartfelt journey through the labyrinth of forbidden love and racism in a Deep South where an entrenched gossip mill and stuffy religious values dictated how people lived, or how they hid their *real* lives.

Reading over what I had written, and polishing the dull spots, I was a bit fearful that my internal feelings were seeping into the piece. I would have loved at that point to write a scathing diatribe on the social, religious, gossip, and etiquette values and rules instilled in residents of small farming communities strung throughout the Deep South. I restrained myself and formed the story into something I truly hoped Ben would feel melded with the emotions I had seen in his eyes.

After I was worn out from nursing the piece from a few quickly jotted notes into a flowing visual and emotional adventure, and then chopping and hacking the extraneous and mundane, I was happy with it, and saddened at the same time.

I can be a sap, and feel that if I cry at a strategic emotional precipice in one of my stories, then there is an off chance that it may have the same effect on some other humans...at least I hope it will.

When I finished reading Ben, Molly, and Zurie's story, I felt a deep sadness and the hint of tears dampened my eyes. This was good writing! I thought.

Well, maybe for lack of extended social contact, I was careening down the treacherous slopes of mental instability...but I did think it was pretty good. I was sure that when Ben and I worked on it some more, the many sagging spots in its literary suit of clothes could be tailored into something first rate.

I picked up the list Ben had given me, and made a few calls.

He came the next morning—Ben, I mean. We went over the piece, and he gave me some worthwhile insights to incorporate. I was beginning to realize that to do the story justice and give it the zest of actual life in this small town, it was going to be a lot of work.

Chapter 28

I called my editor. I had emailed a finished draft of the Mussel Shoals book to her a few days before. I wanted to check in and assess her reaction to the piece over the phone. I tuned my antennae and punched auto dial.

As a successful writer, I had earned the golden chalice of which every aspiring writer dreams—your editor's personal cell-phone number. No longer did I have to wade through hours of miserable and unbearable torment, waiting for the long-awaited call back that most often never comes.

"Jay! How are you!" Her voice was welcoming and concerned as well. It contained a sifting, searching energy. It wasn't anything audibly noticeable. In my previous line of work, public relations, I had developed the finely tuned ability to pick up slight nuances over the phone.

Now, any good editor is half literary expert and half shrink. Authors are, by and large, an odd, eccentric group. Many of us lock ourselves away for hours, days, and months at a time, cut off from ongoing social contact, attempting to create. Sometimes, I think this practice may lead to quirks that an expert editor, dealing constantly with authors, develops a talent for ferreting out.

We covered the formalities of polite greetings and then got down to the nap. Well, maybe nap isn't the right word, but we were about to look deep into the fabric of the literary rug I had painstakingly woven. We were looking for grime and unsightliness that I might have overlooked.

"Well, Margaret," I said, "what do you think? Have you had a chance to read the manuscript?"

"Oh, absolutely. You know how I have always *loved* your work."

She had said *loved*, as in past tense. This was not good.

"I breezed through it yesterday and feel I can comment intelligently because the work is so fresh in my mind."

She let a painful little silence drop. It was another clue. She was readying me, allowing my attention to focus upon her words. A pin could have dropped on her end, and I would have heard it.

"Jay...I...want to be frank. I don't want to give you false hopes. The jump from writing fiction to a real world project is sometimes near impossible for some writers to pull off. What I'm saying is, is that while the piece is informative and interesting in a nostalgic sort of way...it lacks spice, is non-pulsing, and very drab." There was another pause.

"In other words, Jay, I don't want to put you down, but your usual satire and sharp funny exchanges of wit are missing. What we are left with, is a bland sort of docu-drama...it just left me cold and needing a short walk to the pub for a stiff drink afterwards. Can you fix it?" she asked.

There was that unrelenting silence again. I could feel her antennae groping. She was silently assessing my reaction to the bad news.

My mind flashed to the giant surfboard of the literary world. A massive wave was curling threateningly above me. One wrong move, the slightest unsteadiness, and I would be lying in a crumpled broken heap, waiting for those prowling tiger sharks to shred me limb from limb.

"Margaret, I've had some new inspirations to add into the piece. I was calling to see about an extension, to make it over."

"Jay, of course! We want this piece to shine. Polish and shine! Inject your normal writing flare into it. Dress up the characters, give them those larger than life images you do so well. How much time do you need?"

The silence came again, but this time I was ready. "I've already finished a section that portrays the new angle well. I can send it, along with my re-drafted outline, for your ever valuable input."

"Can you send it today?"

There was the investigating tone again. She was wondering if I *really* had it already finished, or was just buying time, like so many writers do, when stuck in the middle of a piece.

"I can send it right now. You'll have it within the hour. Can you call me after you read it and let me know your thoughts?"

"Jay…I'm pretty swamped today…. I suppose…I could read after dinner, and call you when I'm through. How many pages will you be sending?"

"I have over fifty done, but I can send fifty that are clean, and will give you a good idea on the tack I've taken. I think you'll love it!"

"Okay. Send it now, and I promise I'll read it and call you this evening. Will you be up late?"

"Sure! I'm writing like a tornado and haven't been hitting the sack until midnight or later."

"That's my boy! I'll call tonight."

With that, she was gone. Like an all-powerful and fickle wind that first warmly caresses, then turns biting cold, and finally, warm again.

That done, I showered and dressed in some old work clothes, thinking I might drop by the old mill dock and see if Ben and his buddies were fishing. I was planning to stop and see John first.

Chapter 29

I checked to make sure the little house was locked up, walked out, and was about to get into the old Ford panel, when a big, tall pick-up truck came rumbling up my driveway. The guy pulled up and looked at me with an expression that was hard to read.

I've seen these trucks before and always wondered if the guys driving them had a ladder that they climbed to get in. This one had great big shiny exhaust pipes sticking up vertically on either side, right behind the cab. These were the kind of pipes you see on those decked out cross-country semi-trucks with the giant sleepers and the mud-flaps adorned with that chrome Barbie type woman. You know... the one with the pointed breasts protruding at you while you try to find an opening to pass.

He rolled down his window and spat. I guess spat is correct terminology for the nasty boomerang-shaped fluid that came flying out to land on my grass. I contemplated hosing it off while the guy took his time formulating a greeting.

I noticed a huge decal on the truck's rear window. It had four great big bright red letters that I was trying to read backwards. It gave me something to do, while he and I appraised each other. Then it dawned on me...the word was "SKIN."

Tasteful, I thought, as he cleared his throat.

I was expecting another tar-colored boomerang. Instead, some almost unintelligible words came out of his mouth. They seemed to be fighting to flow over a bottom lip that was bulging. I imagined it was packed full of that nasty black stuff so many men down here were fond of—snoose.

"I wanna talk with Lei. She here?"

Now this question surprised me. I'd figured the guy must be looking for odd jobs, or a lost pack of hound dogs... but Leilauna?

I spoke dismissively. "Why would you be looking for her here?"

"Cause this is where she lives, Einstein!" He spat again.

"No. Leilauna does not live here."

I spoke slowly and clearly. I had been taught the technique long before. It worked best when applied to people who had foreheads that angled back severely—Neanderthal types.

"I live here. Who are you?" I asked, my curiosity piqued.

This surprise meeting had been interesting, but now the intrigue ramped up.

"You one a her boyfriends?" he asked, looking down upon me from behind the steering wheel.

"I asked you first."

I was attempting to get down on this guy's level, mentally and verbally.

"You her daddy?" An inspiration had stuck him.

"No."

We stared at one another in silence.

Now this guy didn't look too smart, but he did possess some native cunning. I saw his eyes flick up to the cabin, as if he were wondering whether I might be hiding Leilauna inside, and lying to him.

I figured it was time to get to the brass tacks and acquire some information. "I'm Jay VanVessey. I rented this place about six months ago."

His eyes narrowed to slits. I could see the gears spinning slowly. I was waiting for his name, being that even the backwater rednecks around here were proud of their names, and forever offering them.

"People around here call me Reb."

"Well...Reb, it was nice to meet you. I really must get going. Is there some message I could give Leilauna...I see her now and then...at church." I told a small fib. *God, please forgive me.* "Do you attend? I don't believe I've seen you there."

Now this tack got him flustered. He obviously thought I was attempting to recruit him.

Putting the truck in reverse and revving the engine, he said, "Just tell her you saw me. She knows where to find me!"

With that, he let out the clutch and backed onto my lawn. He revved the engine some more, in a simplistic southern show of masculine power, and took off, sending bits and pieces of green skyward.

Great! Not only did I have a mystery redneck to think about, but I would also now be reminded of him until the grass grew back in the spring. That is, if I stayed until spring.

I was a bit put off, and it took me a moment to remember what I had been up to before Reb's unwelcome visit.

John's place! That's right. I jumped in the Ford and headed towards town.

On the drive down, I thought about the limited conversation I had had with the snoose-loogieing stranger. Why would he say Leilauna lived at the farm she had found for me?

It didn't make sense. I chalked it up to thinking that Reb had probably used a lot of glue, assembling too many model airplanes, in a *very* small bedroom, with no ventilation.

John was in the throes of his early morning silent time. When I walked in, he was reading a novel.

"Wow! When did you learn to read?" I said, smiling.

"First and second grade, just like you, imbecile…only, I mostly like to read very big print and little tiny words." He smiled at his joke.

I changed the subject and got serious.

"I had a visitor this morning. He was driving one of those big jacked up 4x4's and was asking if Leilauna was at my house. He was streaming snoose juice, and revving up his engine. He tore up some of my lawn when he left. Said he was called Reb. Do you know who the guy is?"

"What color was the 4x4?"

"It was red and had two big chrome exhaust pipes sticking up behind the cab, and a great big decal on the rear window that said 'skin' in big red letters."

"Skin?"

"Yeah, pretty classy, huh?"

"Real tasteful. Jay, I know you been living a pretty sheltered life down here. You haven't gotten out much, what with wooing Leilauna and all that *benevolent* work you've been doing on her farm." He winked conspiratorially. "I can think of a dozen trucks that match your description around Mussel Shoals, except without the big decal. What is that about?"

"I have no idea," I answered. "Why would the idiot be at my place, asking for Lei?"

John thought for a moment and said, "Perhaps he knew her from when she played high school sports, and is from another town. Maybe he really didn't know exactly where she lives and was trying to extract the info from you.

"You didn't tell him where her farm is, did you?"

"No, John. Do I look like I just fell off the pumpkin truck?"

John didn't answer. He just raised his eyebrows a bit, emphasizing that southern silence.

"All right," I said, changing the subject, "what have you been up to?"

"Oh, just working my weight down, and wondering when you would show up, with some more of your hair-brained logic." He thought for a moment and added, "Well, logic may be too strong a word."

I mocked him and raised my eyebrows. I wasn't even entering the verbal trap he had so deftly laid. I was beginning to see through John's tactics. It had taken me half a year to learn.

"How's the book coming?" he asked, seeing how I was ignoring his previous sentence.

Now this excited me. I started talking, telling him all about the new direction and Ben's story. Then I swore him to secrecy about Ben's child.

I had piqued his curiosity. "Ben and a white woman? Here in Mussel Shoals?"

Big John's mouth was literally hanging open. I could see his cavernous throat and wondered abstractly just how much deep fried food *had* slid down that dark channel over the years.

I nodded, and let his question dangle in silence. I was learning the power of a well-placed southern pause.

"Man, I think ole Ben must be playing you!"

"No, John...I could see when he told their story that he was about to shed some tears. He can't be acting...I would have picked up on that."

John's big head just swayed back and forth while he pondered. It was great, I thought...me an outsider had some info that John and his vast web of information gatherers had failed to produce.

"Who is she, Jay?"

"*Was*, is the operative word, John. I can't tell you more than that. I think Ben was using a made up name anyway when he told me the story."

"Then it wouldn't hurt you to let Big John in on it, since we've become so close and all?"

John used his puppy dog eyes on me, but my heart was as hard as the four-inch thick armor plating on an Abrams tank.

"Good try, John...but I'll tell you something: those big brown eyes of yours don't do anything for me. Now if I was ten years older, and a black woman, that was still fifty pounds overweight, you might have a chance."

I smiled. His look changed. I thought he was about to pick me up by the collar and shake the answer out of me.

Then he just chuckled one of those deep, thunder-like rumbles and changed the subject.

"How are you and Leilauna doing?"

"I haven't stopped in to see her in a few days. She hasn't come by my place either."

"You two have heated words or something?"

"No, we took a few days down at the Gulf. We checked into a nice ocean-side room and had a great time. We could be ourselves, unlike here in Mussel Shoals. Since we got back, I've been pretty busy writing."

John thought for a moment and asked, "So the marriage thing, Jay, where are you with that?"

"Honestly, John, I think I need some time away from her to clear my head. I was thinking about going home, for a while at least."

"You thinking you can just walk away from that? What if someone else comes along while you're away? Old Reb will no doubt be prowling around. Man, you be kidding yourself! She's got you so wrapped up. It's like you're a heroin addict, and she be giving you your drug. How you plan on giving *that* up?"

"Will-power, John, the same way I gave up drinking." I smiled.

"I've never been one to compare women to booze, but I see *you* could. It seems to me that you've just traded one habit for another."

"You think so?"

"Why don't you just jump in with both feet and quit torturing yourself?"

"*Why is it* that you're always pushing me to marry her?" I said, in a voice raised high. "Is she *paying* you or something?"

John visibly jolted. "NO! Man…no! I would never!"

"John…I'm kidding…I had you so bad!… Whoa! Hah! Hah!"

He looked kind of sheepish and didn't say anything. He was thinking. Finally, he looked me in the eyes and said, "Jay…I just don't want you to go back to where you were when we met. The day your sorry ass drug in here, I thought to myself, now this is going to be *some* fun. You were perfect for my scowl. I wish you could have seen your face when I handed up that warm beer! You sure hung in there though…and gave me all that good advice. I thought I'd have you run outa here in a heartbeat. Boy was I wrong. You were a trooper, and took it on the chin!"

"You sucked down five beers in an hour…."

"It was not five!" I said in protest.

"Hell it wasn't. Listen, Jay! I put all the money you paid for the beer in one empty pocket. I know how many you bought and how fast you drank them! That's my job!"

"Well, maybe it was five."

"Damn straight it was."

"I was really thirsty," I said in my defense. "I get dehydrated when I fly, plus the stress of flying and...and...the food."

"You got any more excuses? All the ones you just listed stink!"

"Sure, I could come up with a lot more."

"Shut up! I wasn't asking you for more. I was asking if you realized how sorry you sound, when you start in giving reasons for drinking like that?"

"I guess now that you brought my attention to it, it does. But you see, it used to be one of my hobbies, thinking up reasons to down a few cold ones."

"Jay, you're a whole different person since you gave it up. Promise me whatever happens you won't go back."

I looked at the big man and saw my best friend. He didn't know, but that was just fine with me.

"I won't, John. Thanks for all the hours, all the talk. You've become a good friend."

"Yeah, well it's been entertaining, I'll say at least that much!"

With that, I smiled wide at Big John and said, "Catch you later. I'm going down to see if Ben's fishing today."

Chapter 30

When I had made it through the potholes and was almost to the parking area near the dock, I saw a huge commotion going on. Ben was in his pick-up and had a long, thin, steel wire attached to the rear end. The line ran all the way out to the dock and up to a beefy wooden spar, with a block and tackle hanging from it.

Ben was revving the engine and spinning his tires. From the way the dust was flying, I could see he was trying to go forward, but the truck was losing ground and being pulled slowly backwards.

I parked out of the way quickly and ran up to see if I could do something. "Ben…what's going on? Can I help?"

"He's a BIG one! Quick, jump in the back! I need a little more weight so I can get some traction!" Ben's eyes were wide with excitement. His breath came in short rushes, like he had been running.

My mind didn't believe what I was seeing, but I followed orders like a fresh recruit in boot camp.

No matter how Ben finessed the clutch, or revved the engine, I could see we were fighting a losing battle. The pick-up tires kept spinning in the loose dirt, and the truck kept edging backwards.

I could hear Ben inside the cab speaking to his machine, like he was attempting to sweet talk a woman into bed. "Come on, baby, I've treated you right. Do this. You can do it for me!"

This can't be happening, I thought.

Then the truck came to a big creosote beam where the dock began, and stopped with a bang and a lurch. I heard the unmistakable sound of something snap, and Ben screamed, "Son of a mother humping bastard!"

I had never heard Ben use any form of foul language. Strictly speaking, I could have described the moment using a much more colorful string of profanity. I didn't tell Ben that. He was obviously regulated by some profane code of ethics.

"What the hell was that?" I was still confused as to what was happening. The excitement seemed contagious.

"That was an old timer, a granddad from times gone by… shit! Damn! I knew I shoulda' bought that heavier wire rope!"

"You can't be serious, Ben. Are you telling me that was a fish?"

"That weren't no fish! That was my nemesis! That ole boy and I go way back! I first broke him off more than a decade ago. And all he does is grow bigger!"

"How can you tell it's the same fish? There could be quite a few giant Gar out there."

"Because," Ben said, as his breathing began returning to normal, "the first time I hooked him, he turned real sharp. He was planning to head downriver and use the current to his favor. He's a crafty old soul! The line when it came tight, was up around his dorsal fin and it got cut.

"When Gar take the hook, and the line comes tight, many times they surface. I can always tell it's him! He has a notch cut into the base of his dorsal fin on the front side. Our story is like old Moby and Captain Ahab. One of these days…I'll get him…if it is the last thing I do!"

We walked out to the dock, and there was something hanging from a spar. It looked like the car hood of a fifty-three Buick my granddad had owned.

Then I realized it was a fish...a monster Gar. Its snout was nearly three feet long, and adorned with an impressive array of vicious looking teeth.

I walked around the thing. Disbelief flew away and was replaced in my reeling mind by awe. This was not a fish, I thought. It was a powerful fabled being from another dimension. Shock dampened my tongue. A revered silence took over, as all of us admired the massive creature of oddity.

"You mean to say, Ben, that the one that broke off was bigger than *this*?"

"'Bout half again."

"You mean fifty percent larger?"

I was astounded, and Ben, who was still a bit short of breath, just nodded. I looked to the others. They were solemn faced and nodding, too.

"How much do you think this one weighs?"

"'Bout four fifty I'd guess. We goin' to put up the scale and weigh him in a bit. You can see for yourself."

"So you're saying that the one that broke off might be over six hundred pounds?"

"Closer to seven...I think. See, we don't know how big they get. Other game fish like salmon are caught in nets. The biggest king salmon on record was caught that way.

"Problem is, Gar don't take to nets. Whenever they get in one, all that's left is a mangled bunch of torn up shreds. They use those teeth see...to cut their way through. So no one really knows how large they can get.

"We believe they live hundreds of years, and like the sturgeon, they never stop growing. They get big fast if they have plenty to eat."

"Are they tasty?" I asked.

"Well, you'll be eatin' some tonight! You tell me tomorrow what you think!"

Ben turned to the others. "I think Jay here brought us some good luck after all!"

"I wasn't even here when you guys hooked them."

"Yeah, but you was comin' on down here. That's what counts when it comes to fishing luck."

I looked at the hanging monster, and then at all four of these old men who were dedicated in their art. They had been catching these giant Alligator Gar for nearly three decades. I admired their patience and ingenuity when it came to conquering such a challenge.

Each of the four's faces were rough and leathery from countless hours in the sun. They wore solid grey hair. To me it was a badge of experience. In some, the posture spoke of a few years remaining.

It seemed to me they were an elite corps of fighters, hunting a powerful and elusive foe. My heart felt no slight honor at having been befriended by them.

I said, "You guys want to come up to my place for dinner? I'll help you clean this monster. Then you can teach me the ways to cook it best."

All four of the old guys glanced quickly amongst themselves. At once, without a word between them, they all began nodding in sync.

Ben spoke up loudly, shouting across the river's surface. He shook one fist in the air in a classic posture of defiance. "One of these days I swear! I'm gonna wrestle your monstrous ass in!"

His words rang out across the water, which was no longer clear and placid. The river ran a deep, dark opaque color out in front of the dock. Farther upstream, clear water was filtering into the area where the battle had been fought. Soon, no evidence of the day's contest would remain.

Chapter 31

My editor, Margaret, called that evening. I waited, holding my breath after I had picked up and said hello. I was waiting for the news that would give me a ride through the stars, or crash me down into a dark and dismal abyss.

"Jay...." She paused, and I didn't say a word. "Jay, I absolutely love it! This new direction you've taken has real depth. The characters are bold and colorful. I feel like I know them already. And that Big John...." She started laughing, "Where did you ever get such a funny idea? He is absolutely wonderful, and the way you've written yourself into the story, interacting with the people, well Jay...it is an absolute lark...a slam dunk. Just keep writing like this, and you'll have another winner! How long 'til you can wrap it up?"

"Well, Margaret...I'm not sure. There is still a lot of information to gather. I'm writing up a storm, but the story keeps morphing as I dig deeper into Mussel Shoal's past."

"Whatever you do, don't rush it, Jay. This has all the makings of a real down home family movie. I'll bet we can partner you up with a noteworthy screenwriter and take this to the big studios. Ever dream of having one of your works made into a movie?"

"Margaret...what author hasn't?"

"You keep this kind of writing flowing, and I'll see what strings I can pull to make it happen. Okay, Jay?"

"Absolutely, Margaret, I am your man!"

"That's my boy! Gotta go! Thanks. Talk soon." With that, she was gone.

I spent the next few days visiting and writing. I didn't see Leilauna.

I planned to make Ben and Molly's story the centerpiece of the new direction I was taking on the book. The other stories would be like planets orbiting around the rising and setting sun of their long friendship.

I also decided that instead of placing the people's experiences down on paper in a documentary style, that I would mix the bits and pieces of the work into each other. I mean this was a community right? These kids grew up together, some of the fathers worked at the old mill together. The ideas came to me, flashing faster than my two and sometimes four fingers could hit the keys.

The piece was unfolding and blossoming into a community taken by storm, altered drastically by a monetary boom and an influx of un-local personas through a revolving door—a flashing, glittering, powerful door that had slowly stopped turning over twenty-five years ago.

In the tragic wake of the boom, some of the best and the brightest young people exited the stage of a once sleepy little southern town that had nurtured them from birth.

The new direction and my excitement with it began morphing the fairly bland work I had previously done into something that was a vibrant, living, breathing organism.

Leilauna was in the back of my mind. I was no longer just a writer of made-up fiction...I was working with real flesh and blood and a freight train full of human emotion. I was more fascinated by the piece as the days went by.

Visiting the folks on Ben's list, I met some very down to earth and poignantly touching people. I think after that, I was a slightly different person. I felt my story was a piece I had been destined to write. I loved it.

I had been so preoccupied with the writing, with the interviews, the fishing, and visiting John, that Leilauna had drifted farther back into my mind. I was no longer preoccupied by thinking of her constantly...I felt I was beginning to be cured of the craving and need she had so deftly built inside of me.

I thought about the strange visit by the big four-wheel drive truck and the snoose-spewing Reb. I had meant to tell Leilauna about the guy and pass on the message. It hadn't seemed important, but for honesty's sake, I determined I should pay her a short visit, then come home and work some more on the book.

There must have been something in my voice, a questioning tone or something.

"You don't trust me?" she screamed.

I had never seen or heard Leilauna act like that. It was unsettling.

"Leilauna...I was only saying that he came looking for you. I never said I didn't trust you, or that you knew him."

"But when I told you I didn't know who he was...you looked at me in disbelief." She was standing in her kitchen, with her hands on those wondrous hips.

"No! That wasn't it at all," I said. "Don't read something into my look that isn't there."

Perhaps suspicion *had* shown on my face. I hadn't been given any reason to think she knew the guy, yet I'd seen the slightest flicker in her eyes when I'd asked about him.

"Please, Leilauna," I said, "just let it go. Let's not talk about it now.... How are you?" I asked, attempting to change the channel.

"I'm fine. Except I miss seeing you. Are you...is there something...are you upset with me?"

"No Lei, I'm not upset. I've been busy on some fresh perspectives in the book. And I've been fishing for Alligator Gar! Plus, you seemed worn out from our days away...I was, too." I smiled, thinking about three full days of intimacy with Leilauna. I wanted more, but not here like this. I was tired of hiding how we felt.

"Yeah," she said dreamily, "it was sure nice being away."

"I've got to go home...for a while anyway," I told her. "I hope you understand. It's been almost seven months. They were wondrous months, Lei."

She rushed up and clung to me. "I can't think about being here without you!"

"Come with me then. I've asked enough times."

"I can't, Jay. I can't leave the children...they *need* me!"

When she said the word "need," her voice became slightly shrill. I began to wonder whether it was actually that *she* needed the children, not the other way around.

"You could come for a week and see how you like it. That way, you wouldn't have to miss Sunday school. Or better yet...why don't you ask someone to sub for you, and then you could come for two weeks?"

She looked thoughtful, and said she would consider my invitation.

I went home to work.

Chapter 32

I WAS AWAKENED when I felt her slip in beside me and snuggle up. Sometime before dawn, she woke me again. This time, I needed her tenderness.

At breakfast, she pleaded for me to stay another ten days, so that she could get used to the idea of us being apart. I thought of consenting, and determined silently that when her next "low love cycle" began, I would depart.

I finally agreed.

That evening she came back. It wasn't two in the morning like usual, it was just after dark, and she had brought a basket with dinner and a bottle of Merlot.

I hadn't had a thing to drink in months and liked the way I felt. I wondered of her church's beliefs on drinking and asked.

She replied, "Jay, I'm only trying to accept a more moderate philosophy and doctrine. Perhaps my church *is* too rigid. Will you share some wine with me? It could signify a new beginning for us."

It all made perfect sense—especially when she took off her long coat and I noticed she had on her lavender Cashmere sweater dress. It was my favorite, and she knew it. It was made from the thinnest sweater material I had ever seen. It clung to her curves and made her appear to be naked, with lavender skin.

She looked to me when she took off her coat as I took the garment from her and admired what was underneath. I saw in her eyes a confidence, sureness, as if she had expected my wandering hungry eyes to rove over her every curve.

We ate lightly and turned in early. Her high love cycle had kicked in. I would be in paradise for as long as it lasted.

Even with the wiles of her tender touch grasping me in my wine induced state, I had the presence of mind to remember to renew, repeatedly, my vow to leave.

She came to me nightly for ten unbelievable evenings that ran into the early hours of morning before we collapsed and slept like the dead.

Chapter 33

THERE WAS STILL work to do on Leilauna's farm, and so I stayed busy breaking my time between writing at my place and working on hers.

The past week had been a dream. We were getting along splendidly, whether we were vertical or horizontal. My resolve to leave had weakened. I was vacillating again. I found myself mentally somewhere between my resolve, and her tender wiles.

Leilauna had gone to town, intending to pick some things up at the grocery store for dinner. I had been cleaning up some old rusty barbed wire that was stored and making a mess of the barn loft. A piece of the nasty stuff tore through my glove and into my hand. "Shit!" I said aloud, when I took off the glove and saw the damage.

Now any fool knows that rusty barbed wire cuts are a nasty prelude to something even worse—lock-jaw!

I quickly went into the house, intending to find some peroxide or another form of antiseptic with which to clean the cut. I also needed bandages.

I looked through the medicine chest and found nothing of help. I started going through the drawers and found a little first aid kit. I picked it up, and what lay beneath it startled my naiveté.

There were pregnancy test kits. One was lying under the first aid kit. There was a white paper bag, and inside I found five more and a receipt for ten.

What?! My reeling mind screamed. I had never thought of *this* scenario. Was Leilauna trying to get pregnant?

My mind raced through the unpleasant memories I had purposely stored in mass volumes. Memories of children I did not like, and of babies that threw up and had nasty, messy diapers. I thought of the bodies of formerly striking women. Bodies that had been altered forever, terribly changed, for the sake of having children.

I had resolved early in life to forego the questionable blessings and virtues of children. Sure…millions of people would tell you it was the best thing they had ever done; however, if I had a dollar for every time I had sat on a barstool and listened to the miserable account of divorce and child support from one of the countless victims of this much lauded trap, I could quit writing and retire comfortably.

"Never!" I had said valiantly, whenever my ex-wife had brought up the subject. It was one of the things that had led to our minimalistic sex life and our unhappiness. You see, she had changed upon hitting thirty. A little bird began speaking into her ear. It was infecting her with the questionable belief that children would make our miserable marriage better.

We had decided before getting married that children were not important, that our freedom and financial health *were*. Then all of a sudden, it changed. She had desperately wanted children. I had vehemently refused. It was the icy cap to an already frigid and long-failing relationship.

She gave me an ultimatum: It was have children or get divorced. I had been hovering on the precipice of that decision for nearly a decade. Her words were the weight that cast me over the edge.

My mind reeled...Leilauna testing herself for pregnancy?

I heard her car coming up the drive. I quickly bandaged myself and put things back as I had found them.

Leilauna came in that night. I didn't even look at the clock to see what time it was. When she snuggled up to me and began taking it into something more than nestling, I said, "Lei honey, I'm tired. I was working late and just got to sleep. Could you just hold me?"

She sighed heavily and complied. In the morning, she wasn't cooking breakfast as usual. She had gone while I was still sleeping.

I was fine with her absence. Before I had begun working on revamping the Mussel Shoals book, I would have weakened, thinking she had been so close and I had turned down her advances. It had been a first for me. I hoped she wasn't too put out.

I got up and made some oatmeal with chopped apple and raisins with toast. I sat down with my new, evolving outline and ate while I worked. Sun broke through the clouds and it looked to be a pretty, clear blue day.

Chapter 34

"John, I'm heading home. I don't know for how long. I want to thank you for all your support, your advice...even though I didn't heed a lot of it. It was still important."

"Yeah well, when you get my bill...we'll see if you're still so positive!" he said.

"Hey, if you ever get up Seattle way with the wife, come and stay at my place. I've got an extra room. I wouldn't charge you much for rent. I know it would be difficult tearing yourself away from this cash cow you tend."

He laughed, but it wasn't the same. Our acquaintance had grown into something much deeper. It spoke loudly, leaving the question each of our minds was silently asking: when would *this* life bring us near one another again?

"Jay, I've got to say...I enjoyed your visit here. Damn, brother, I was getting flat out bored till you showed up! My bet is on Leilauna though...you won't last three weeks in Seattle! You be crawling back needing some of that drug of hers!"

He laughed, and I could tell that even though he was being lighthearted, there was an underlying current of sadness. We both felt it.

"It's been great, John," I said.

I walked out of his bar, not turning around to wave or say a last goodbye...I was a lonely drifter in one of those old westerns. They just ride off into the sunset, without ever looking back.

The next day I was thirty-seven thousand feet above our planet, streaking across the sky in a jet, heading to Seattle and *my* home.

I am not embarrassed to admit, I was fleeing from the brewing storm of potential marriage, children, divorce, and child support. I had made my escape. I was a free man, even though I was not necessarily a happy one.

Chapter 35

I HAD BEEN back in Seattle for three weeks. If John and I had bet, I would have won.

There were women I could see, friends I had made since becoming a noteworthy author. Some of them were quite fun and very loving. I stayed home mostly, went for long contemplative walks, and worked on the book. I really didn't feel like going out and socializing. Leilauna and the fond memories of our months together lay on my brain like a smothering pillow does on the face. Sometimes...I found it hard to breathe when I thought of living any extended length of time without her.

The work on my book had become complicated. I needed to re-structure the entire project to add in my new passion—the stories I had collected from people who had daughters and sons leave Mussel Shoals and follow the bands.

Ben and I spoke on the phone regularly. He was gathering some additional bits and pieces to help me round out the book in hopes that it would become a living, breathing story, full of vibrant characters and the roller coaster of life. I truly believed the drab project, as Margaret had described it, was morphing into a heartfelt journey backwards into a piece of previously undocumented history.

I was pretty happy. My mind drifted back to the seven months with Leilauna hourly. I missed her, but I had decided that I was not going to fall into the marriage trap without a pre-nup.

If she truly loved me, as she regularly professed, she would happily be bound to me without dreams of some future financial bounty if things went sour. I had seen just enough of her mysterious low moods that I was being cautious and treading as though the weak, translucent ice of our relationship could fracture at any time and dump me into frigid, deathly water. That thought kept my emotions cool and in check.

I worked and ate and walked. I did little else.

I called Leilauna a couple times a week, just to let her know I loved and missed her. She was warm, and yet I could feel something when I talked with her…I couldn't be sure, but it seemed she had an antennae that was groping the air, attempting to feel whether or not I was weakening.

Chapter 36

I HAD BEEN in the study writing when I heard the familiar and lightest creak of the front door hinges. I poked my head out of the study door and looked down the hall. I froze in shock at the sight before me.

She was taking off her coat, setting down a fairly large rolling travel bag.

I was stunned. How had she gotten here? How had she gotten a key? Who was teaching Sunday school? My mind raced.

I rushed up and swept her into my arms; tears filled my eyes.

"Leilauna! I'm thrilled you finally made it. Let me have a good look at you!" I broke from our embrace and held her hands at arm's length.

She was different in a way upon which I couldn't really place a finger. She had always been voluptuous, and she seemed even more so...voluptuous I mean...*perhaps it was because I hadn't seen her for so long.* Her face glowed, and her eyes possessed a sparkling clarity, a brightness that struck me to the core. .

I acted like she was late for dinner, not that I hadn't seen her in nearly two months. I didn't want to make a huge issue out of a little thing like that. She was here, and my heart sung because of it.

"Are you hungry? I could fix you something."

She said nothing.

I noticed a smoldering intensity in her eyes. I saw them flash. As she touched me, I felt that electricity again, the static had actually sparked between us. I looked at the blue arc and wondered where this woman had come from. She had turned my sequestered world into a dream-world. I had lived that dream in my sleep, a hundred times before.

I woke in the morning wondering whether she had been a vision. I felt for a warm spot next to me. I couldn't really tell. The bed was a shambles.

Then I smelled bacon and coffee. Rolling out of bed and onto my feet, I quickly brushed my teeth, then went down the hallway and into the kitchen. She was there, the woman I had longed incessantly for.

She was making us breakfast.

The next couple of weeks, I spent with Leilauna in Seattle, traveling and introducing her to the wonders of my home state. She was impressed.

We rode the ferry across Puget Sound, and spent a few days on the Olympic Peninsula. Stopping for a night in Port Townsend, a Victorian seaport built in the 1800s, the blues festival was in full swing and I had been fortunate enough to find a reservation at a gorgeous Victorian mansion, sitting on a couple of acres of well-tended and verdant gardens with paths. The ornate home was full of antiques and bits of local history; it made a wonderful bed and breakfast getaway in a quaint and colorful historic port city.

We visited the west coast beaches, took long walks, dug clams, and gathered oysters. Then we jumped a ferry at Anacortes and went to Orcas Island for a couple of days, staying in a Greek shipping tycoon's former mansion, which had been converted into a five star hotel.

Most of all we enjoyed each other's company and being free to love one another, without worrying what other people watching might think.

After nearly a week of travel, we were ready to settle back in at my condo and play house. I had never been happier. I believed that she would fall in love with our new life here together.

It didn't happen quite the way I had envisioned.

Daily we would take long walks along Alki Beach. One day, while sitting on our favorite driftwood log, she began her attempt to woo me back to Mussel Shoals.

"Come back, Jay. Let's go back to where we used to be. On the farm…in the two houses."

"Stay here with me, Leilauna. This is my home. I want to stay here for now."

"Sure, baby, I'll stay a little longer, but you may wake up alone one morning, and I will have gone back home. Then if you really can't live without me, you'll have to come to me there."

"To live separately? To sneak around in the woods so the neighbors won't see? All the while, you're teaching Sunday school?"

"I love those children…I was called to do it…to teach them, to love the Lord and to know right from wrong."

"It's wrong for us to have to live that way! To be looking over our shoulders, worried what other people might think."

"I can't make you understand how important they are to me. I can only tell you that teaching them is." She brushed a few strands of dark hair away from her eyes and looked at me intently.

"So that's it? I'll just wake up and you'll be gone?"

She didn't say anything. She just took my hand and led me up the beach. The wind played with her shirt, outlining the curves I was so fond of. I tried to think what it would be like being alone here without her, if she left. The thought cast a pall over an otherwise beautiful spring day.

Leilauna stayed with me in Seattle for over two weeks. In that time, we experienced a love-drenched honeymoon, without being formally married. I felt betrothed to her. She did not feel the same way.

"Why, Leilauna, is being married so important to you?" I asked her one day.

"Jay, without the legal bond of marriage, it is too easy for a person to just walk away when times are not as rosy as they were in the beginning. How many relationships have you had without marriage, and how long did they last?" she asked. "Were you the one to call it quits?"

She had asked a lot of questions. I hoped I could remember and answer them all.

"I've had five or six relationships since my divorce," I said. "Some lasted a month or two, others a year or more. Yes, I was the one to walk."

"You see! That is exactly my fear! What if I gained some weight and you didn't find me attractive anymore?"

"I will always think you are scrumptious."

"But you can't be sure! What if you awakened one morning and just thought, this has been fun, but I'm ready for something new. Where would that leave me? Don't you see my fears? Being bonded in matrimony means that you must work through the low spots. Many people who aren't married just give up and walk away during the frustrations. I can't live like that anymore, Jay. I need commitment. I need your trust."

"I would never walk away from you," I told her. "You hold my heart in your hands. I am vulnerable to your specialness and beauty."

She looked hurt. "That is easy to say, but the history of your past relationships makes me wonder."

"Bonded" was a key word. It rang alarm bells in my brain. I had been bonded and branded once. I had sworn it would never happen again. Now, as I looked into her wounded eyes, I weakened.

"Leilauna, I love you. I...I'm just not ready to marry... without a pre-nup. Is that piece of paper so important? With it, you get what you desire! I hope you understand."

"I desire your trust, Jay VanVessey," she said, angry now. "By forcing me into a pre-nup, it makes your love conditional and says you don't trust me! I've told you time and again, I won't do it that way!"

We ate lunch in silence, then went for a walk at Alki beach. Gulls swam through a wispy blue grey sky, chirping their strange, forlorn language. Ferry boats crossed the shimmering Sound towards the Olympic Mountains, Bremerton, and Winslow. Joggers ran, and bicyclists rode. A warm spring wind brushed the dark strands of her hair. She had not spoken, other than to acknowledge my words with a subdued smile or a nod of her head. I felt the sudden energy shift. I may be blonde, and I have been called densely insensitive, but her cool mood would have been obvious even to the seagulls sweeping overhead.

Finally, looking to me, I saw that rare momentary flash of coloring in her eyes. Her emotions shone like jeweled highlights.

Then she said, and I will never forget her words, "Jay...I want you always. I don't wish to play hardball with you. Free will *would* be best for both of us...but either way...."

Then she smiled like I had never seen her smile before. Her face showed multiple emotions; it was a bewildering mix of determination, knowingness, and love, all mixed up together. I had no idea at the time what she meant...even though I was trying desperately to understand.

I attempted playfulness, saying, "My life's desire is to fulfill your desires, Leilauna." I leaned over and kissed her ear.

"I have to go. Why don't you come down for a couple weeks, Jay? It's been three months. Mussel Shoals misses you. I will miss you before my plane leaves the ground...I'll be missing you."

"When you come...to visit...I'll go with you...we'll go to the Gulf like we did before. Only this time, let's stay a week...what do you think?"

I didn't respond. I was looking at her intensely, attempting to read her true intent. I thought I could see mist forming in her eyes.

"I need you in Mussel Shoals, Jay," she said. "I need you home with me." She turned her face away and stood. Can we...go now?" she asked, her voice weak and trembling lightly.

"Sure," I said, wondering about her mood.

"I'd love to visit. When should I come?"

"Anytime, Jay...anytime.... Soon?"

"Real soon. I may sit on your lap on the jet," I said playfully.

Chapter 37

I HAD NO way of knowing what would befall me in Mussel Shoals the following year. People speak of the sixth sense and of premonitions. At that time, I felt nothing but abounding joy.

I was back in the Deep South.

I had John to visit and fence wits with. There was fishing with Ben and his handful of Gar enthusiasts, and the finishing touches to Leilauna's farm, which we worked on together.

I worked on the book, with Ben helping. He had a never-ending fountain of stories from his five decades of handyman work in and around Mussel Shoals. He exhausted me with information. I struggled with the task of fitting the best of it into the book. The trying part was deciding what parts would fit well into the story line, and what would muddle it.

All in all, the project was coming along nicely, and I hoped to wrap it within a month. What I would do then...I had no idea.

I hoped fervently that Leilauna would come back to Seattle and stay, at least for a while.

Summer was in full swing. Leilauna's farm was becoming storybook tidy, and there wasn't a lot to do. We spent our free time picnicking and swimming at our special place. We shared quiet dinners and a bottle of wine now and then. Life was what I thought of as real and ideal. I longed for these pleasant days to last forever.

When I first stopped in to see John, he looked and acted surprised to see me. I'm sure he had heard I was in town, but he made me feel like it was a complete shock to him.

"Hey man! I sure am glad you didn't take me up on that three-week bet…I didn't think you had it in you, Jay."

"What, John?"

"The resolve and will power to stay away from that handyman project you been slaving away on." He winked.

He meant Leilauna of course. "Handyman Project" was secret code. He was speaking in the language we used when the checkers club was in session.

"John…I may have a few surprises left for you," I said. "I haven't shown you what I term sheer resolve yet…maybe someday when you're older and wiser, you could handle that lesson!" I winked back.

"It's great to see you. You sure are looking trim! That new health regime you've been on is paying big dividends!"

I smiled to myself, thinking about how I didn't miss those big neck inner tubes he used to be packing around.

"John, I never thought it would feel so good to be back. I hate to admit it, but I missed this sleepy little town. The big city hustle grows on a person. The small town peacefulness takes root. I particularly missed the ambiance of your establishment. I see the nail is still sticking out on the seat of that thing you call a bar stool."

"Well, fool, you could sit at another."

"This one grasps my consciousness. Not only was I sitting on this stool when we first met, it's also well broken in, from all those sessions we had."

"You get my bill in the mail?"

"You're kidding, right?"

"Yeah…I be messing wit' you!" John smiled wide, and those big, gorgeously straight white teeth shone. How I had missed that smile! It was a thought foreign to me, missing a man's smile. I had experienced missing a woman's before… but this was a definite first. It opened my eyes wide to a friendship that was *really* in its infancy.

I decided that if I was going to spend time in Mussel Shoals regularly, I should see John other places than here at his bar.

"Hey John…why don't you and the wife come to dinner at my place? We've never really socialized outside of here. Maybe it's time?"

"She would like that, and her name is May Ellen. Don't forget to say them both. Her name is not May, and it's not Ellen. It is May Ellen. She gets *real* particular about that."

"John, you have scribed the name May Ellen into my consciousness with a very sharp point. It is imbedded so deeply, I'm sure I could never forget."

We laughed lightheartedly and settled on Friday night. It was two days away.

The two of us talked about my time at home and how the book was progressing. Then we fell into a comfortable silence, as we had often times before.

Finally, I said, "John, I'm going down to the dock and see if Ben's fishing. I'll catch you later."

Chapter 38

BEN WAS ALONE at the dock. When I walked up, his outward appearance seemed happy, but for some reason I felt it was put on, like he was acting out a show just for me. There was something in his eyes that spoke of an uneasiness... I couldn't place the feeling running through me. It was something like a premonition...but I had always looked down upon that superstitious nonsense.

Ben was as gracious as ever.

"Jay! I thought sure I'd seen the last of you. Most visitors when leaving Mussel Shoals swear an oath...never to return to this little forsaken...."

His voice trailed off into nothing. I knew he was well past seventy and figured he was experiencing one of those mental burps that leave our minds uneasy; knowing there is more, deep in the gray matter, waiting to surface...but not quite ready to.

He started out of what seemed to be deep thought and said, "Jay ...you're back! I didn't expect to see you again. Last time we talked, you were saying you thought you could wrap up the book without another visit to Mussel Shoals."

"Well, Ben...you know, the best laid plans and all."

I couldn't tell Ben that I had come back because Leilauna needed me here.

"I was getting kind of bored in Seattle. I kept thinking of your nemesis and wondering whether you would catch him without me."

"Oh! That old boy and me, we have a run in about once every year or two. I don't expect him back for a while. You know though, Jay, I'm real glad you came down. There's some things I want to say...I guess now's as good a time as any."

Ben looked out across the blue water to the far bank and beyond. His voice had an ethereal quality that made me take note. This was not casual conversation. Embedded in his words was a definite message. I just didn't know what it was at that time.

"Sometimes, Jay," he began, "life will throw you a stiff twist. There are times when a person wonders what his purpose is, and why he's here, and why things went the way they did. Do you understand what I'm trying to say?"

"Not really, Ben."

Ben stood and went to his cooler. Opening the lid, I noticed him bring out two bottles of a locally produced dark beer. "Will you join me Jay?"

The question seemed innocuous...yet in the future, it would ring in my brain like a Sunday church bell...over... and...over.

"Sure Ben."

"Well, I already told you about Molly. That for *me* was one of those things I'm talking about. I often wonder *why* it all happened. The memories are pleasant enough...but there is also such sadness laced through them, it takes away the joy and leaves a melancholy threaded through me often times.

"My wife passed some years back. I lost my best friend. The old house just isn't the same. I go home and the walls seep memories of her and the children. I think sometimes of selling the place, but can't bring myself to do it. It's like my roots have grown so deep there, I can't just pull up and walk away."

Ben gazed out across the river. I could see the melancholy...so thick it was a flavor. It showed in his movements, and in his eyes, and in the grayness of his dark features.

"Then all my children moved away from Mussel Shoals. The wife and I wanted something better for them and made sure they all went to college. All the children decided they wanted fresh beginnings away from Mussel Shoals. I can't say I blame them...the Deep South is still pretty backward when it comes to black folk getting a good start in life.

"I see the kids a time or two during the year...I wish it were more, but they're busy working and raising families. So, old Ben...he just passes the days on this dilapidated dock, remembering irreplaceable days gone past, days that were happier and more fulfilling.

"I guess I'm wandering a bit, Jay...I am at a loss for how I should say what I need to." He paused. "I like you. I don't want you hurt, or to end up like me, alone and with nobody but some old men similar to myself as company.

"I am glad you're back though! Whatever happens, Jay... the end is all that matters. If you are happy with where you end up in your golden years, then you've been a success. You may go through some horrible times...times you think are trying to steal everything—your self-esteem, your wealth, your sanity—from you...times that may look like you're drowning with no one near to throw you a rope. But if you keep the faith and believe, you'll make it through. I know you will."

"Did any of what I just said make sense to you?"

"I understand, Ben," I said, nodding, but really I *didn't* understand. I was still trying to take in and process all the information he had shared and how it related to me.

Ben obviously thought that it did, for some reason unbeknownst to me.

"Jay, I'm driving up to southwestern Tennessee tomorrow. There's a place up there that is just the most beautiful. I've been longing to see it again. I haven't gone in quite a while and just decided it's time. I was wondering if you would like to go with me? We could take my pick-up so you could enjoy the scenery on the drive."

"What place, Ben?"

"It's called Second Creek. I spent my whole life in these parts. I never have seen a place anything like it. Why, they have trout up there that will fight until your arm gets tired. The water in some of the deep holes is so blue, you just want to stop and stare into it for a lifetime...so beautiful...so peaceful...like no other place in the world. Jay, you should come.

"I was thinking we could stay for a couple days. I've got a tent and all the gear...we could camp out. I could pass some more stories to you by the fire, teach you to fish for something less elusive than Giant Amazonian Gar. Maybe there's some stuff still in this old head that would make that book of yours even better than it is."

I hesitated, thinking about being away from Leilauna for two days. If I had to choose between Ben and her, well you see what I mean. But I felt the pull of his invitation...I was drawn. There was something beneath the surface, I mean Ben's surface, that was trying to show itself to me. I had no idea what it was; I could only feel it.

Ben had become a good friend. He seemed to need some company. I had almost decided.

"Will it be just you and me, or are some of the other old guys coming, too?"

"Just you and me, Jay. I think we should spend some time…get to know each other a bit more. I think that would be good for both of us. Considering everything."

Again, that far-away look came into his eyes, the softness I had seen before. I had seen the same look in his eyes more than once, when he had been silent, gazing out across the river. The time I had asked of parents who had lost young loved ones to the bands. Another time it had shown when he had shared his heartbreaking relationship with Molly, their daughter out of wedlock, and her running away with the bands.

"Okay. I can drop what I'm doing and go. What time do you want to get started?"

Ben looked me in the eyes and the brightness of a younger him returned.

"I could pick you up at six thirty…it's light by then. No sense in driving in the dark. Would that be too early?"

"No. I'll be ready."

"Good….that's good…just fine."

"Jay, I want to find Zurie. I don't know how to begin… searching…you know. I'm an old man with few financial resources and little of my younger investigative intellect and drive left. Jay, you have all that."

He looked at me, almost pleading. "Tell me, if I help you on this book you are writing…if I help you make it into something astounding…a story that will bring not only the tragedy here in Mussel Shoals to light but will also garner you critical acclaim…will you help me find her? Zurie…I mean?"

"Sure, Ben," I said, nodding. "I will be glad to help you find your daughter…if she's still living."

"Promise me. Give me your word that no matter what happens between us, you will help me find Zurie."

"I promise you, Ben."

Ben reached out and grabbed my hand. We shook on our agreement. He had a strange knowing look in his eyes, and I couldn't help feeling that somewhere in my future, I would understand his look. But today, right here, I did not.

We sat for a couple hours more. The river flowed quietly before us. No giant fish darkened the water and nothing exciting happened. The two of us were comfortable saying nothing and taking in the scene.

I left as the sun was getting low in the sky. As I turned my rig around and started down the pot-holed road, I waved to Ben. He didn't acknowledge or see me. He was just staring out across the water, seemingly lost in thought. The picture of him, silhouetted against the darkening water that showed the colors of sunset, stayed with me for a time. That picture comes back to me now and then…and I wonder why. Why it is so ingrained into my memory?

Chapter 39

I SWUNG IN to see Leilauna on my way home. My heart picked up its tempo in anticipation.

When I pulled up to her house, she was watering her garden and looked adorable in shorts and a haltertop, wearing one of those straw hats the farmers wear.

When I rolled to a stop, she sprayed my truck with the hose. The window was open and she got me right in the face. She then broke out laughing. I mean she was bent at the waist, her humor causing joyous convulsions. She thought it was all really funny.

I feigned a pout. She stopped laughing and traded in her humor for a dismayed look. She actually believed that she had hurt my feelings.

I got out of the truck and walked to her with slouched shoulders. All the while, I was buying time, plotting, getting her to drop her defenses, and hopefully the hose, so that I could grab it and get even. In my family, water fights were taken on with the serious and calculated cunning of ancient combating gladiators.

My ploy worked, after a fashion. She let me up close but kept the nozzle in her hand.

I took her by the waist and trapped her arms. Then I tickled her until she writhed and dropped the hose. I had my hand in the right place and grabbed it. Once I was armed, I broke free of the manipulated embrace and dowsed her till she screamed with hysterical laughter.

She had nothing to lose; she was already soaking wet. She jumped on me and bent my wrist with both hands. In a moment, the two of us were both equally drenched.

I was laughing so hard I could barely stop.

I grabbed her in a bear hug and walked towards the corn, then bulldozed some stalks with her behind. I went onto my knees and gently set her down on the green and yellow bed.

"Jay VanVessey...what in the world are you up to? Ruining my corn like that?"

"It's not ruined. We can still eat it."

"You're going to bruise it!"

"Maybe a couple of ears...I'll buy you some more."

"They won't be fresh...you know how I like my corn fresh!"

Just then, I saw her weakening. It might have been the laughter, or the water, or my dashing looks...but I definitely saw her weakening.

She said, "Here?" in disbelief, and I nodded. I think she might have, if it weren't for a very loud sounding truck coming up the driveway.

Jumping up and looking at the mess we had made of each other—we were muddy and soaked—the laughing was obviously over.

The tall, red 4x4 with the chrome pipes and the huge decal pronouncing "SKIN" was coming out of the trees.

"What the hell?" It just tumbled out...I couldn't believe my eyes.

"I told you he's been coming around, Jay. I've tried to give him the brush off every time. I think he's either very hard of hearing or has the thickest head I've ever seen."

"Let me handle this," I said, exuding manliness.

"Are you sure, Jay?"

"Absolutely!"

I walked out of the corn and the garden gate. Reb's eyes narrowed down to those little slits I'd seen before when he saw it was me.

"Can I help you?" I asked.

Out came the tar colored boomerang. I was expecting it this time, so I wasn't caught by surprise. The disfigured words also came as expected.

"I come to talk with Leilauna."

Leilauna was hiding in the corn patch.

"She isn't handy right now. Would you like me to give her a message?" I asked politely.

"Didja tell her I wasa lookin' fer her?"

"Yes Reb…I passed on your message."

He eyed me with suspicion. Then, without saying another word, he backed up and revved his engine up just like before. I was feeling a bit of deja vu when he spun his tires and threw some sod skyward on his way out.

Leilauna peeked between some cornstalks and said, "I sure am glad you were here, Jay. I just can't seem to make him understand I am not interested. I just don't get it!"

"Leilauna…with that type, probably only a baseball bat would enlighten him to your true feelings." I shot her a mischievous look and said, "Now, where were we?"

"Oh! That's right!" Up came the hose in her hand and she gave it to me good. Or maybe bad would be a more correct way of putting it.

I always kept a change or two of clothes in a backpack in the Ford. The humidity and the dirty work I always seemed to be doing made it a necessity. I grabbed them and followed her into the house. She threw me a towel.

As I changed, I began thinking about the visitor and about leaving Leilauna alone for a couple of days. When I mentioned my concerns, she said, "Just a sec, I want to show you something."

She went into her bedroom and came out with a double barrel 12 gauge shotgun. "This was part of my inheritance," she said. "Gram taught me to use it. One barrel is rock salt and the other is full of double-aught buckshot. Just depends on how serious things are, as to which trigger I pull."

"Please! Always remind me to keep on your best side, baby!" I looked at the old double-triggered shotgun, eyes wide.

Then she put the gun back in its resting place beneath her bed and began stripping her drenched clothes off and tossing them in a basket. I watched without blinking.

Leilauna made me feel that I should never leave her again. Gone were the high and low flows of her intimacy and tenderness. She was full on...well, she was absolutely fabulous, just great, I thought. I needed that after nearly two months without her luscious and inexplicable company.

I had been back in Mussel Shoals less than a week, and my life seemed idyllic.

Chapter 40

Awakening in Leilauna's arms, I tried not to stir her. I was basking in her tenderness and comfort. I had longed for this while I had been away in Seattle. Now here in her arms, all seemed perfect.

She rustled our warm blankets, which were permeated by her scent. It flowed up into my nostrils and I knew this woman...I knew...I was addicted to her tenderness, and to her big, gorgeous, brown eyes, which fluttered open sleepily. "Jay! You're here...I was dreaming we...we were separated...by a distance. I couldn't find you...then.... Oh, I missed you when you were away in Seattle!"

"I missed you, too." I pulled her close. "Ben asked me to take a short trip up to Tennessee for a couple of days. Can you live without me?"

"Why would *Ben* ask *you* to go up there?"

Leilauna wore a quizzical look, as if this were some puzzle, almost assembled, and the last piece was missing.

"He's going up to camp and fish. He said he would like some company, and that he had a few more stories, stories that we could fit into the book and round it out."

"Oh...." She looked at me intently.

"That's it? Fishing and storytelling?"

"And camping out," I said.

"Sure...only...I was hoping we would be *inseparable* here, on your short visit...but if you want to go with Ben, it's fine."

"Leilauna, I would much rather spend time with you. I just feel that Ben needs some company on this trip. I'm very close to wrapping the book...and he has been an invaluable help." I looked to her with beseeching eyes, hoping she would understand.

"Jay, I don't pretend to own you. You are free. I have never pretended when it comes to that...."

Her voice trailed off and left a thread of longing hanging between us, as though she had dreamed of owning me.

Chapter 41

BEN SHOWED UP the next morning at six thirty sharp. I was packed and had a thermos of piping hot black coffee ready. I poured a second cup, handed it to him, and we carried my gear out and threw it into the back of his pickup.

Before long, we were on the open road heading towards new and exciting adventures. I felt like I was six years old again, and finally beginning a long awaited fishing trip with my dad.

Ben whistled softly. We didn't say much, just enjoyed the view and the comfortable feeling of friendship.

Second Creek would have been called a river in *my* home state. Here in Tennessee, a river has to be at least a hundred miles long to be called a river. So this beautiful, blue, flowing creek was in some places a hundred yards across.

Ben parked the truck, and we stepped out into a wonderland of wildlife. A warm breeze caressed the trees and the water whispered along verdant banks.

Walking through the hardwood forest, we soon came to a big, deep blue hole. The water had an entrancing aquamarine color, like a glacier shearing off into the sea. Sunlight played through the flowing liquid, casting a myriad of bright, rippling reflected light on the limestone creek bed.

"I like to camp here," Ben said. "There are some other areas designated for camping, but you have to put up with people walled into little slots. I know lots of people go from the city to a campground like that and are happy because they are in the woods. Me...I like the solitude and beauty of *this* spot. What do you think? Should we set the tent up here?"

"Perfect, Ben," I said, looking around. "This place is something from a dream. I never would have ever imagined it could be so breathtaking. Thanks for bringing me up here."

Ben smiled at me. I had always liked his easy going nature, but understanding this side of him gave the man a depth I hadn't taken in before.

"It's still fairly early. If we wait much longer, the trout won't be hungry. We better get busy catching our dinner."

We walked back to the truck, and Ben pulled out two fly rods, already set to go.

"Here you are," he said, handing one of the rods to me. "Ever fly fish before?"

"Not in the true sense," I answered. The orchestra of casting had me nervous. I had seen people do that in movies and in real life, but whenever I tried, I was invariably a tangled mess before I caught anything.

Ben could see my apprehension, and said, "Come, it's just a soft, easy rhythm. If you relax and just enjoy the day, you'll get the hang of it."

We walked to the water, and I let go of my nervousness, breathing in the scents and basking in the sunlight. I thought about Ben's words and realized he was right. To just *be* here was enough. It really didn't matter if I caught some fish, or I tangled my line. I had no place to go. No worries to think about. I relaxed as Ben gave me the motions without having the line out. We worked together for a few minutes, and he said, "That's it...you're getting it.

"The main thing is to make sure you have enough space behind you so that you don't get fouled on your back-cast.

"If you walk up the creek about a hundred yards, you'll be at my favorite spot. Now the big ones are crafty. If they see your shadow in the water, or hear you knocking rocks about with your feet, they will not bite. So you have to sneak up on them. Okay?"

I nodded. Ben looked at me and said, "Well, what are you waiting for?"

"Thanks for teaching me the rhythm, Ben." I turned and walked parallel to the water, but far enough from its edge not to cast my shadow into it. I also heeded his words and picked my footfalls carefully...I was the stalking, sneaking predator...an aboriginal hunter seeking dinner. I was a kindergartner fly fisherman. I was happy as hell.

The campfire's dancing light played on Ben's dark face. We sat there enjoying the sun's waning light and the way everything surrounding us changed color. Words were few between Ben and me since arriving here. Nature's music and visual bounty seemed to be enough for both of us.

As the fire burned down into a low bed of glowing coals, Ben pulled out a well-used cast iron grate and set it level on the rocks that surrounded the fire.

Our catch was laid out on a wooden cutting board. The fire's light played golden red upon the silvery bodies of three gorgeous fish. Ben had caught the largest, a trout bigger than I had ever seen in person. Sure, you see that kind of fish on the cover of magazines and on sportsman shows on TV, but in person? My fish were much smaller. They were dwarfs beside Ben's 21-inch beauty.

"I think the big one will feed us both, Jay. Shall we put the other two in the cooler for breakfast? Nothing like fried potatoes with onions, fresh eggs, and trout for breakfast."

"Sure, Ben. I've had a great time today. I wasn't sure about coming up here with you…thanks for persuading me to come."

Ben said nothing for a while as he placed some flour and salt in a paper bag, shook it up, and then put the big fish in the bag and tossed it lightly some more. Pulling it from the bag, the trout was no longer speckled silver but a dry, dusty white.

He placed it in a big cast iron frying pan, which had already been coated with olive oil and butter, and the fish began to crackle lightly as it cooked.

"Jay, when I was in the war, I saw some ugly things… things that change a man…forever. There were times I thought I may never come home…*so* many of us didn't.

"In and through the worst of it, in the darkest, most terrifying moments, I held onto my faith that it was not my place to be devoured in the consuming furnace. It was a fire that ravaged many dear friends of mine.

Ben looked to the darkened river, as if he could find the words he was wanting to speak, among its rustling current.

"In the end…I made it home in one piece.

Somehow I had been spared physical agony and maiming injuries." Ben stopped talking and leaned forward lifting the big end of the trout a bit, looking to see how brown it was I guess. Then he began again.

"Jay, when I look back upon those days…they come to me as a nightmare does. They don't even seem real anymore… like a horrible dream that leaves you upon awakening, trembling and sweating from the uncertainty and the fear.

"How, I do not know…but through all that, I was spared. I can't help but think it was my faith that protected me. My belief that I had a life yet to live, and it would not be over until I was very old. I have that same feeling about you, Jay. Something tells me that no matter what happens, you have that same faith, that same belief.

"Hold on to that strength, Jay. If you do, it will carry you through the darkest of times...."

When Ben's voice trailed off like that, his words were pounded into my brain as if by sledgehammer.

Ben was silent. He turned the fish to reveal a golden brown color, and it smelled wondrous. My stomach growled.

"Looks great, Ben," I said. "And thanks for sharing your thoughts with me."

I really didn't understand at the time how his words related to my life, yet his advice made sense, and touched me in a way that would be difficult to explain. There was a form of bonding that had taken place between us when he spoke them. A feeling rose inside of me; it swirled around like the smoke from the fire, wispy, full of flavor, melancholy mixed with other feelings—fulfillment, happiness, and a wistfulness gnawing at the back of my mind. It was a desire to better understand what this quiet man was *really* attempting to impart to me.

We were silent while Ben took the fish out of the pan and threw already cooked potatoes in with some onions, quickly stir-frying them into savory splendor.

"Grab a plate," he said, not looking up from the fire.

As we sat down and were about to dig in, Ben spoke again, softly. This time he looked me directly in the eyes. "Jay, I like you. I would never have brought you here...to this very special place otherwise. Know that I am your friend, okay?"

"Sure, Ben."

We ate without saying anything more, then stared at the campfire's flickering, dancing light. The river ran in my head. The stars overpowered my vision. I was lost in a trance...a hypnotizing dance of nature and newfound friendship.

"Jay, you gaze out into the stars and you soon realize that we are, as people, so miniscule," Ben said, finally breaking the silence. "Why, an asteroid could come here and wipe out this entire planet...we would be powerless to stop it. You understand what I'm trying to say?"

"Not really, Ben," I said, shaking my head and smiling.

"Well, sometimes forces in life, they sweep us away. We don't even understand how it is that we've lost our footing...that we are no longer in control. The most important thing when you get into a situation like that—like I just described to you—is that you are in the hands of a caring person...someone who can see you through the tumult. You know that type of friendship, and your life has been a success.

"Jay, I want to find my daughter Zurie. I have no idea where she might be. A promise to me is something sacred...an oath to be fulfilled come hell or high water. Did you mean it? Will you?" Will you truly work to find her?

I looked at Ben and saw the decades of pain in his eyes. It was a suffering that spoke volumes to my heart. I responded by saying, "Sure, Ben, I'll help you find her."

"You promised right?" he asked, his big dark eyes searching mine.

"Yes, Ben," I said, nodding solemnly. "I promised"

He smiled that mysterious, all-knowing smile I had seen before—the one filled with humor—and I wondered...I wondered what depth he knew that I had yet to understand.

Chapter 42

BEN AND I had been back from our camping trip to Second Creek for a couple of days. Leilauna and I were painting the new railing I had built along the high side of her front porch.

"Jay, with you back and not working the handyman truck, it won't be long before people will be wondering what you *are* doing. Maybe we should start being seen together a bit. Now that you aren't a tourist, it wouldn't be looked upon the same way."

"Tourist, heck! I'm leasing the farm and have made some good friends here! It sure should be acceptable to any busybody taking note."

Leilauna smiled. She had a little sparkle in her eyes. It looked like mischief, but I couldn't be sure. She said, "I was thinking of having a small party here, just some close friends. I wanted them to see all the work we've done to the farm. I want you to be here, Jay. You will have to be discrete though, no intimacy in public...understand?"

"Oh? I think I could keep my hands off you for a few hours."

"What about your eyes, Jay? The way you look at me sometimes...it's like you're dying of starvation and I'm a juicy filet mignon. Sometimes I'm afraid you'll start drooling."

"Be serious...am I that obvious?"

"Totally." She laughed and came up and rubbed into me. "Actually, I like the way you look at me. Her eyes smoldered as she gazed into mine. "But it wouldn't be appropriate during a social gathering."

"I can be the definition and picture of appropriate. Trust me."

"That's what the big bad wolf said to Red Riding Hood... just before he drooled."

She laughed again and I joined her, thinking about the two of us seen mingling at a social. Things were definitely improving. Leilauna was loosening her strict moral code a bit. Perhaps it was those bottles of red wine. If that were the case, I would begin ordering it that way—I mean, by the case.

It wasn't a large group, just a few of Leilauna's friends. I asked John and May Ellen. They came, and we entertained outside under a cloth shading tent and the trees. I barbecued chicken and spare ribs. Leilauna had taken care of the rest.

Compliments on the food and the farm abounded. Leilauna shone like the full moon over placid water. She was so beautiful, and now I was no longer being kept locked away in a closet like an embarrassing deformity. My heart welled with joy. I think I was happier than I had ever been before that day.

Seattle and my condo seemed like a far off world of make believe. This place, this strange little town in the Deep South, was growing roots into me. I could feel them.

Chapter 43

One day, Leilauna posed the spontaneous idea of a picnic.

"Okay," I said. "Where would you like to go?"

"We could borrow the little rowboat Ben keeps at the dock. There is a really nice little side channel up the river just a bit. Would you like to see it?"

"Sounds fun. Should I ask Ben about the boat?"

"Would you? I feel kind of funny talking to him about it. I really don't know him that well. It also looks better for you to do it. Bring some shorts. There is a great little sandy beach, and in the cove, the water gets real warm."

Leilauna was in the kitchen making sandwiches for our picnic lunch. I was outside, scrubbing out an ice chest that hadn't been used since our trip to the Gulf. I heard her exclaim, "SHIT!" which was unlike her. I had never heard her talk like that before and knew something was wrong.

I rushed inside and to the kitchen. She was standing, wide-eyed, looking at her hand. It was dripping crimson onto the counter and cutting board.

"Oh my God!" I blurted. Grabbing some paper towels, I grasped her hand with them, afraid to look. Dabbing the blood away, I could see a large, deep cut across her index finger. "I'll get the first-aid kit!" I rushed to the medicine chest in the bathroom, and she followed a moment later.

Washing the cut under hot water, I realized with relief that it wasn't as serious as the blood had made it appear. "You must have nicked a vessel for it to bleed like that," I said, my voice filled with relief.

"We should probably call off the picnic," I said. "No sense in going out when you're injured. We can stay here, and I'll nurse you back to health." I smiled, trying to take her mind away from the pain.

"Don't be silly," she said. "I've suffered much worse. Just put some Neosporin and a band-aid on it and let's go. That damn salami was tough, and the knife blade kind of bent, and my cut went off course right into my fingertip."

It was a dreamlike afternoon. The sun spoke out between scattered, undulating cumulous clouds. A slight breeze blew across the river and into our smiling, expectant faces. We were embarking upon an adventure together, just she and I. The thought was new and exciting for me.

I climbed down the ladder to the rowboat first and then steadied Leilauna as she stepped into the little craft. I had practiced rowing as a kid, and the rhythm came in even, hypnotic motions. Ripples lapped the wooden hull and added notes into a sky that sang with the waterfowl living along the shore and in the woods along the river's many little back channels.

Leilauna glowed. I reveled in sharing this time with her, and my mind ran forward thinking of the blanket we had tucked away in the picnic basket.

"Head up towards that point, Jay," she said, showing me the way. "The little bay is just around it."

As we neared the headland, Leilauna stood up and looked back downriver. I was looking the same direction and noticed that the town had disappeared behind a sweeping bend.

Quickly, she shed her dress, and I noticed she had her black one-piece swim suit on beneath. "Don't you look scrumptious," I commented, sweeping my eyes over her entirety.

"Jay VanVessey, don't you ever tire of leering at me?" She wore a teasing smile, and in that moment, I found myself thinking, *She is everything I need. The perfect woman for me.*

"Never!" I shot back, with exaggerated certainty.

She turned towards the stern and then dove into the river. I was in shock!

"Leilauna, get back in!" I hollered. "The Giant Alligator Gar...you shouldn't be swimming here!"

"The Gar?" She laughed lightheartedly. "Who's afraid of the big bad Gar? I'll race you to shore!" Then she began stroking powerfully towards the headland about a hundred yards away.

I picked up the oars and began turning the boat in the right direction when I noticed a change in the water. It had gone from sky blue to the color of clay, and there were swirls. Then Leilauna screamed. I saw one of her hands rise into the air—then she was gone.

I rowed frantically, looking for her, screaming her name over and over. I was shaking uncontrollably. There was nothing.

The Giant Gar! I couldn't believe it...it was true!

The water took on a different color where she had been. It was no longer the color of clay; it had turned a muddy red. And then, slowly, as I searched in vain, it began to change back to its usual clear, silky blue gray. Soon it was placid; the murkiness was swept downriver by the current.

She was nowhere to be seen. There was only silence, frightening silence, broken only by the pounding drum of my heart pulsing in my ears.

I went for help. I rowed like a banshee, screamed up the ladder, and sprinted to my truck. Throwing it into gear, I tore down the potholed road with frenzy. Tools in the back of the old panel were flying around like popcorn cooking. The truck leapt in the air, bucking. It was a wild mustang; I power-slid it onto the blacktop, fishtailing like a maniac.

Chapter 44

SLIDING TO A stop in front of the sheriff's office, I jumped out and flew around the truck, not even closing its door. Bursting into the tiny office, I yelled like a lunatic, "Leilauna! She's been attacked by a pack of giant Gar!"

A very overweight man in an official county uniform heaved himself up to a standing position behind his desk. "Slow down, son! You are making no sense. Take a deep breath and tell me what has happened—and please pause between your words so they do not come out as gibberish."

Then he sat back down.

The sheriff looked at me a little funny when I exclaimed, "Leilauna's been eaten by a pack of giant Alligator Gar."

When I explained that we had been going on a picnic, he raised his eyebrows.

"So, where did all this take place?" he asked.

"Up the river from the old mill dock!"

"Well, let's go take a look...at the scene. I mean, where she disappeared." He lumbered from his chair and we started out of his office. He gathered up a couple of deputies on our way out, and we all went down to the dock.

Sheriff Tate and crew followed me to the old rusty ladder where the rowboat was tied. "We were heading to that spot up river," I told him. "She said there was a nice little cove there around the bend. She said it was a good picnic spot." I was not speaking well. Stress does that to me—and sorrow. My mind still reeled in disbelief.

The sheriff and his deputies exchanged glances that I didn't understand. I was still in shock—faint and nauseous. My hands were cold.

The two deputies climbed down the ladder and into the boat.

One yelled up, "We got blood here, Chief!"

What? my startled mind screamed. *There was no blood! In the boat! NO!*

I looked over the edge of the dock and there was her dress, stained with a few red blotches along the hem.

"What in the world?" I blurted out. "She cut herself making sandwiches for our picnic...I didn't see her bleed in the boat though...or on the dress. How in the hell?" Words were tumbling from my brain onto my tongue in a jumble.

"That's what I'm thinking, Jay," he said. "How in the hell?"

"Do you want to give me your statement now?"

"What statement?"

"Your explanation of the disappearance of Leilauna Delan!" Sherriff Tate said, as the deputies climbed back up the ladder and handed him the dress.

"I just told you! We were going on a picnic and she jumped in the water, saying she would race me to the other side."

"And did she take this dress off before she jumped?" The sheriff held up the dress, a look of reproach in his eyes.

"She was wearing her swimsuit beneath it! She was in swimming clothes!"

"When did she take off the dress, Jay?"

"Just before she jumped into the river."

"Right...okay. Why don't we take a drive up to your place, and then to Leilauna's, and look around?"

"Shouldn't you get some divers and search the river for her?" I asked, frantic. "Wouldn't that make more sense?"

"Jay, I consider myself a fairly easy going fella. I don't want to sound pushy, but I have a gut feeling on this one. It's telling me we should look over your place of residence, and Leilauna's. Now do I need a warrant? Or will you take me there without one?"

"If you think that's what's important, yes I'll take you there. What about the river?"

"One of my deputies scuba dives. I'll send a couple of them down there in our boat and have them scour the place for anything meaningful. In the meantime, let's you and me take a little ride. Okay with you?"

"Sure." I had agreed to go, but it made no sense to me at all. What would we find at the houses, when the disaster had happened at the river?

My mind screamed out a thousand questions. I broke down, crying silently on the way up the river road.

She was gone!

The fucking Gar!

I would become a Gar hunter. I would punish them for taking her.

Chapter 45

I opened the door to my little house, and Sheriff Tate rushed past me like a linebacker after a quarterback. He went into the bedroom, then the bathroom, he came out with some bloody paper towels. Then he went to the kitchen and looked around the rest of the house. Tate found a knife and more blood in the kitchen and the pile of paper towels I had used to staunch the bleeding of Leilauna's injury.

I had come to the realization that I was either still in shock, or this was a very vivid nightmare.

When Sheriff Tate slapped a set of cuffs on me from behind, I knew I wasn't dreaming. The cool steel bit painfully into my wrists.

"What the hell is going on here?!" I yelled.

"What's going on here, Mr. VanVessey, is that you're under arrest for murder in the first degree—the murder of Leilauna Delan. You have the right to remain silent...."

Sheriff Tate's demeanor changed with the snapping of the cuffs. I struggled a bit. My mind staggered drunkenly through the events just unfolded, attempting to ascertain what had made him think I'd murdered Leilauna.

He pulled out a nightstick and said, "Quit struggling and attempting to resist, or I'll knock you down and drag your sorry, perverted ass into that patrol car! You hear me, Yank?"

He also said something like, "You think we're a bunch of southern dullards down here. You think we can't see what you've done? All the while working on that beautiful young lady's farm...your twisted mind was plotting to get under her skirt! When she rejected you, it put you off the deep end!"

I started to blubber something, and he gave me a dose of stink eye that instantly shut my trap. We rode to town without another word between us.

At the jail, I was forced to strip. I was sprayed with some kind of liquid I could only imagine was a delousing and pest controlling agent. I prayed silently to wake up from this hellish nightmare and at the same time that I would not be allergic to the chemical.

I was booked. My mugshot was taken. And lastly, I was thrown into a cell by myself.

I was frightened and relieved at the same time. I had heard enough horror stories about northern white boys visiting the Deep South, being framed for a crime they did not commit, and then being thrown into jail cells with giant black homosexual inmates named Bubba. The Bubba's in the stories always had a dislike for white Yankees who had been framed and arrested for murdering innocently beautiful young Sunday school teachers.

My mind raced in frantic circles. What should I do? Then I remembered watching Perry Mason as a kid. I had one phone call! Who should I ring up? This was a quandary. I thought of my sister, but we had fallen out years before... no, that was out of the question.

In my youth, when trouble had landed me in a tight spot, I had always called my mom and dad. They were dead and couldn't help other than through spiritual support.

JOHN! I could call John! I even knew his phone number at his place of business. I made the call.

On the other end, there was nothing other than some forced grunts and breathing. When I asked him to come to the jail and see me, there was dead silence for a while. I thought we had been disconnected. Then I heard him say, "Okay, I'll come after dinner. I got to think on this awhile."

Great...my only *real* friend here in Mussel Shoals was unsure. Even John thought I had done Leilauna in! *SHIT!* I could only think in profanity—a string of filthy, desperate words ran tumbling through my brain, dominating the space between my ears like a freight train meeting another freight train head on in a dark narrow tunnel.

I was sick to my stomach, frightened, and in shock. I had thought the grueling divorce from my ex-wife was brutal. This was just beginning, and I was already worn to a frazzle.

Surely they would come to their senses. There was a simple explanation for the blood on the dress. Leilaua's cut must have started in bleeding again. She must have used the hem of her dress to wipe it off because she had nothing else. Yes! That was it! My brain craved an answer... an answer that would buy me my freedom and mend my rapidly fraying nerves.

I sat on the edge of the bunk and cried for Leilauna. I cried because the dream of a woman I had once known and loved was gone. The fragile path we had secretly threaded together was no more. I was alone without her. I sobbed in anguish...not for myself but for her tragic, brutal end. In grief so black, it blurred and darkened my vision, I wept. I could not believe she had been stolen from me.

Chapter 46

John was the first to come see me. He was an odd sort of green beneath his normal black. I had never seen him like that before. He looked afraid to begin speaking. He looked as though he was wondering how he could have misjudged me and then befriended me.

"John, it isn't true!" I said. "I don't know what is going on here! We were going on a picnic. She jumped into the water, and all of a sudden it changed color and became dark...a muddy gray. Then she was drug under screaming. John, you have to believe me. I love her! I would never harm her!"

I started sobbing, and I guess the big man thought I *might* be telling the truth.

"Look, Jay. I know a good attorney. He isn't cheap. Do you have money?"

I nodded.

"A case like this will begin at fifty grand and could go much higher. Justice is speedy here in Alabama, so it will be wrapped within a year. Appeals are swiftly ruled on as well."

He paused, then said, "I just have one question, Jay. How did the blood get in your house and the boat? Everyone in town is talking about it."

"She cut herself while she was slicing some salami for our lunch," I said. "That is the truth, John. I'm living a nightmare, and I can't explain any more than I have."

"Are you back to drinking, Jay?"

"I swear I am not."

"I believe you. But it's crazy—everybody is saying...to believe she was eaten by a pack of Giant Gar."

"John! I saw one hanging at the old mill dock. It was huge! Ben lost one way bigger! It had to be them fucking fish."

I don't usually say the "F" word. Well, I mean I don't say it unless I really feel like I'm being...screwed. And I knew I was. There was no getting around it.

"The attorney I know...you want him?" John asked.

I nodded, attempting to wipe the tears from my eyes and get my voice under control.

"Okay. I'll send him down to see you."

"Thanks, John...I mean it."

"It just ain't right, Jay. I don't know what happened. It's just hard to believe...here in Mussel Shoals and Leilauna... such a beautiful young woman...."

John's eyes bore into me. His piercing, scrutinizing gaze drove me to despair.

I knew he still wondered....

I couldn't say anything. I just looked right back into those big brown eyes. I was shaking like a leaf...my face was screwed into an ocean of anguish. I choked out, "John... I love her!" I started sobbing again.

"Stiffen the lip, Jay. Get a hold of yourself. I believe you, man! I believe you."

I looked up to him. He was an angel standing there. He was my big, black guardian angel. I was stricken by the thought, *Here is my best friend.*

"John, you don't know what it means...your friendship...believe me...."

"Shut up, man! You know Big John don't take on friends lightly. My heart's with you, Jay. We'll get to the bottom of this...somehow."

The attorney friend of John's came. He introduced himself. I liked his name it was clean and clear and carried restrained power. His name was Robert Cole. He was a rumpled old guy with a bush of gray hair and a mustache that you knew covered a too-large lip. His ears were doggedly long, like my Great Grandmother's had been. He had clear eyes, clear and sharp; they bore into mine like a marine drill sergeant about to make you drop and do fifty. His step was lively. I waited in anticipation for him to open his mouth and speak, figuring he would sound like everyone else around here. When he spoke, I was pleasantly surprised. His voice was clear and plain. It possessed a dignified inflection and tone, unlike most people south of the Mason-Dixon line. He was, to my astonished ears, missing the languid southern drawl.

"Jay, I have to be honest with you," he said. "The evidence is pretty damning. The blood, the dress, and your house...well, you know how it was found. The fact that you were her handyman, and that you are so much older."

He flipped through some papers in front of him. "The prosecutor has taken the evidence and is building his case upon the assumption that you became obsessed with Miss Delan...and that your obsession drove you to kill her when she rejected you."

"But she *didn't* reject me!" I said. "We were lovers. I am going to tell you the entire story, no half-truths. No untruths."

"Jay, that is the only thing that has any chance of breaking the prosecution's case. If one lie shows up in your testimony, you are finished! Do you understand me?"

I nodded. "Yes.... We were lovers, I mean not only in the physical sense. I asked her to marry me. She wanted to be married you see, but I told her she would need to sign a pre-nup. She refused. So our relationship went on in secret.

"Finally I flew to Seattle. You see, I was weakening...I needed time...and space to think. I was home in Seattle nearly two months when she came unexpectedly for a visit. It was a complete surprise. She just showed at my condo and let herself in. I didn't even know she had a key.

"So before she left to come home, she asked me to come back to Mussel Shoals for a while, and I agreed. I've only been back less than two weeks...the fucking Gar devoured her, in the river."

"Did you see any giant fish?" he asked.

I shook my head. "No. I just saw the water darken. Then she screamed and was pulled under. She had her arm stretched into the air. Then it was gone. The water turned from kind of a clay color to a rusty, reddish brown. I rowed frantically around and couldn't see her. I could only think to get help. So I went to the sheriff."

"Jay, no one will believe that story," Mr. Cole said. "There have *never* been any recorded fatalities from giant Gar. Some people claim to have been attacked by them, but none of those reports have ever been substantiated by the authorities. I don't really believe it either." He leaned forward in his seat. "What *really* happened, Jay?"

Those piercing eyes above the too-large mustache bore into mine once more.

"I just told you!"

He stared at me. It was the appraising look of a detective. Someone who has been lied to ten thousand times, and after that time, begins to believe that everyone is lying. His look made me squirm in my chair.

"Jay, the story is far-fetched. I have to admit, something in your eyes tells me you had nothing to do with her disappearance, that perhaps it *was* an alligator or a Gar. Still, whether I believe *you* isn't important. What the jury believes is."

"Do you think this farce will really make it to trial?" I asked.

"Jay, the woman is missing. You admit to being the last one with her. There was blood—*her* blood—in the boat and at your home. There is also the dress...and the knife, and your DNA everywhere."

"I don't know anything about this kind of case," I said. "Don't they have to have a body to charge someone with murder?"

"Not necessarily," he said, shaking his head. "The circumstantial is so strong on this case. They do need something...what the prosecutor *has* is the minutest piece of Leilauna's skin. It was stuck to what he is calling the murder weapon...the knife. That tiny speck of skin *is* the body, Jay...or what the prosecutor will say is left of it."

He sighed. "Jay, you have to understand...even if Leilauna vanished in the river, it doesn't explain how her blood got all over the place. They didn't find it in your truck. That is the only point in our favor."

"She cut herself while slicing some salami for our sandwiches," I said again. "The ones she had been packing for our lunch. I was outside, I heard her exclaim something loudly, so I rushed into the house. She had blood dripping from her hand. I went into the bathroom for the first-aid kit and she followed me. I bandaged her finger."

We talked some more, and he told me to get some rest and that he would be there tomorrow for the arraignment. I asked him what that was about, and all he said was, "It's about pleading NOT GUILTY, Jay."

Then he left. There was no way I could sleep. When I did manage to drift off, I had nightmares and woke in a surreal world of fiction that was, upon coming into my senses, not fiction at all. I waited all night for morning and what it would bring.

Chapter 47

THE TRIAL WENT on in the fashion you would expect from a backward, religiously oriented swath within the Deep South. I was the foreigner. I had killed a beloved and innocent Sunday school teacher. I would be punished. I could see it in every one of the juror's eyes as the prosecution spewed on and on and on.

It wasn't long. The clock had barely moved when they came back with a verdict of guilty in the first degree.

I prayed fervently to a God I had never recognized before. I prayed that I would wake from the nightmare.

My desperate pleas went unanswered.

As the year rolled to a close, I soon resigned myself to the inevitable. This was no dream. I was not going to wake up. My only avenue of escape was the oasis—that promised land, the island within a storm: the shelter of a successful appeal.

My appeal was briskly denied for insufficient cause.

The nightmares were more than disturbing. I awakened from them in a state of panic set in by emotions so strong, it felt like a massive electrical current was running through my body and about to explode it.

Becoming conscious, I would be drenched in sweat and weak in the knees. I was alone in a cell...being held 'til the day they would walk me down the corridor and strap me in to the chair.

I had lost all hope.

Chapter 48

I HAD FEW visitors. The case had been plastered across the nation. Everyone believed I had done it except Ben and John. I saw them regularly. But now that I was on death row, everything was done with a piece of bulletproof glass between us.

Ben visited me most often. I had decided I would complete the Mussel Shoals book before my gruesome grand finale. Ben was an immense help. He showed up for a visit one day, and as we were sitting there talking about the final polishes on the book, he held a small piece of paper up to the glass partition. I squinted because the writing was very small. It said: *Leilauna sent a picture.*

I gasped.

Ben held up a photo of Leilauna. She was standing in Grand Central Station, beneath the digital date-keeping display. The photo had allegedly been taken the week before.

I looked up from the picture to Ben's face. He wore a sad sort of smile...it was the smile of someone who is suffering quietly. It was a knowing smile. It said he knew some dark secrets that had been kept from me. He just sat there with that enigmatic look, nodding his head.

I was outraged. My heartbeat spiked and my blood boiled. How could he be so insensitive? If this was a joke, it wasn't even remotely funny.

"What the hell is this?" I asked, restraining myself against an attempt to dive through the impregnable glass.

"It's a game, Jay...and you lost." Ben spoke quietly, softly. He then he held up another note: *Sign all of it over to the Mt. Zion Family Trust, Jay. Leilauna comes back. You are then a free man.*

I looked at Ben in sorrow, in disbelief.

"Look, Jay, I've seen and talked with her. She told me about the 'please bite my neck thing.' How could I know that?" He shook his head. "Man, I like you. I don't want to see you take the walk. Just do what the note says when your attorney visits. He can take care of it all."

He rose from his chair but then sat back down. "Promise me when you are free," he said, "you'll help us find Zuri... like you said you would. Jay, I want to find my daughter. I need your help."

"What?" I mouthed the word in horror. I was speechless and rapidly going into shock. Could it be true? Could it all have been a game? Her sick, freakish game? *NO!* my mind screamed. Then, as I cooled, the pieces began to fall into place.

What if it were true? My reality...my memories of her would not allow that thought to take root. It couldn't be! Or could it?

Then he left.

Ben had left me blinded by a blur of disbelief. Could it be true? What did I have to lose? Once they fried me in the chair...my money wouldn't do anyone I really cared for any good, unless I directed where it went.

Why not Mt. Zion Family Trust? I thought. They had rented me the little farm...fond memories abounded when

I thought of the months I had stayed there. Why not? I could think of no reason not to sign it all over.

I hadn't spoken to my sister, who was my nearest living relative, in years. Not since the death of my parents and her absconding with the family wealth by taking care of my parents in their senile years and power of attorneying most everything to herself. If I did this, she would certainly be deprived of inheriting my royalties.

I didn't dare believe Leilauna was still alive. I wondered what kind of gruesome mental game Ben was playing...giving me a shred of hope when there was no chance.

I did, however, want to give my bitch sister a gigantic middle finger. And I wanted my freedom...my life.

So I did it. I signed it all over.

A few days went by, and all of the sudden Sheriff Tate was standing outside my cell with the prosecuting attorney and the judge. I also noticed three very large deputies standing against the walls. I wondered what the hell was going on. I sure hadn't expected to see those three again.

The judge cleared his throat and began in that deep baritone voice I had heard so many times during the nightmares that had shredded my sleep the past year.

"Mr. VanVessey, there has been a terrible mistake. We feel that we owe you our most sincere apologies. You see, Leilauna Delan has appeared here in Mussel Shoals. She is alive and well! So, Mr. VanVessey, you are a free man. We are very sorry for the trouble we've caused you, not to mention the financial expense and the embarrassment." All three men shook their heads solemnly.

I looked at the three of them like they were out of their minds. I was speechless. They must have seen the look on my face because the sheriff started talking in a soothing voice. "Jay, this is not the time to do something foolish. You are a free man. A year and a half of your life has been stolen from you. I am truly sorry. Keep calm. You can walk out of here right now! You are a young man—you have the rest of your life in front of you. Please be reasonable and calm."

"Calm! You want me to be CALM?" I nearly shouted…but not quite. At the thought of my FREEDOM, I began to settle down, realizing if I didn't there was a chance they would just keep me locked in that atrociously depressing cell.

I accepted their apologies, gathered my personals, and walked out the door of the state prison alongside the sheriff, who had graciously offered to drive me back to Mussel Shoals.

I had no idea what I would do when I got back to that stinking little town. On the way there, I decided that I had better call my lawyer and revoke the power of attorney I had signed on his behalf. Sheriff Tate graciously let me use his mobile phone. I also called my editor Margaret and asked her to wire me some funds. She asked me for an option on the story…*my* story—the freaking tragic, wrongful arrest and imprisonment for the murder of a woman I would have happily died to protect. I agreed. That done, I thought about what I would do next.

When we rolled into Mussel Shoals, I said, "Drop me at John's bar, Sheriff."

Once there, I pushed my way through the door and a flood of memories flashed through my mind. The big man looked like he'd seen a ghost. "Jay? What in the hell?"

"They let me out, John. Leilauna isn't dead after all. She turned up here in town…."

"I don't understand. What are you saying?"

"I'm saying that I've just spent the last two and a half years of my life being fucking flimflammed out of nearly everything I own!"

John was in complete shock, too. Neither of us could believe that it had all *really* happened.

"Call me dense, but I don't have any idea what you are saying!"

So I sat down and gave John the quick down and dirty. I then went to the bank, picked up my wire, and took a cab to the airport.

I didn't give a rat's ass if I ever saw Mussel Shoals, Alabama again.

Chapter 49

I WAS ONCE again fleeing. I was flying away for the second time from a little town in the Deep South. It was a sleepy northern Alabama town that had thrown me some very nasty knuckle balls. Mussel Shoals had become a God forsaken wasteland of misery for me. It was the one place on Earth that had managed to knock out the two front teeth of my self-esteem, along with my entire life's purpose.

I had struck out in love and financial security in Mussel Shoals. I was fleeing the bastard of a mother-humping, fuck of a town, with my life...and just barely with my life.

She! I had begun to think of her in that way. *She* was no longer Leilauna. *She* was the she-devil, the bitch who had cast me adrift...the one who had sucked out my marrow and left me for dead. *She* had deftly played the game. I thought it was a freakish game...a game that *I* had lost, without knowing I was playing...without even having an idea, not understanding that I *was, and had all along*, been, her sacrificial pawn....

On the way home, sitting in first class, I belted down a few beers. *I* had earned them! I justified going back to the place I had promised Big John I would *not* go.

I rationalized moving away from my private oath of sobriety, and the promise I had made to my best friend. I thought, what *was* the difference? I knew he would kick my ass if he found out that I had reneged on my oath to him. But he would *never* know. I was flying over two thousand miles away from his dirty, despicable, and shabby little bar. How could he reach out and touch me from there? I thought confidently.

I had happily given up drinking in order to have a chance with Leilauna. Where had it gotten me? I asked the Great Universal Unknowingness. I had just spent *sixteen freakish* months in a concrete cell, wishing and praying for some *miraculous* piece of evidence to turn up that would set me free. That miraculous piece of evidence that would save my ass from smoking and popping like an unattended sausage in a red hot skillet. Thoughts of the electric chair had broken the solace of my dreams into shreds of dismembered insanity, threads of suicidal mania, it came in my dreams...there was no escaping it. In my dreams...it still came. When it did, I woke shivering, cold and hot at the same time. I dreaded the nightmares until the fear of them kept me from sleep.

So I began drinking again, at odds with my oath. I drank hoping I could go to sleep. I willingly indulged so that, even though I was no longer in a dank, uncomfortable, and depressingly un-day lit cell, I could enjoy a few hours of no-REM sleep...and I eventually paid.

I ordered another beer. I fought my way through the mental haze of fear and misery the past year had wreaked upon my previously robust countenance. I was, I realized, a shattered wreck. The beer was not helping me focus. I was still desperately working to understand what I had been through.

By the time I got off the plane, I had no intention of renting a car. I jumped into a cab and braced myself for the $120 fare.

I was drunk. The stewardess had begun looking at me funny after I had downed the eighth beer. I could have *eas-*

ily handled more. I was celebrating, damn it! She had no idea where I had *freakin'* come from!

My condo never looked so good. I passed out on the bed.

In the morning—or it might have been afternoon, what did I care—I took a long walk along the beach and ate out. I called friends and visited. I met new women. I was actually a celebrity. "The man sentenced to death row by mistake." I should have been happy. Everyone thought that I should be happy. I pretended I was in front of them.

I was not.

Only four people knew it was no mistake: me, John, Ben, and Leilauna.

My editor Margaret called and proposed to set up a nation-wide promo tour. She offered to set up interviews on television and radio. Interviews any aspiring writer would have gladly sacrificed their left nut to obtain...well, if they were a male writer, that is.

I declined, saying I wasn't ready for the exposure, and I wasn't. "Maybe next month," I said, attempting to pacify her.

I am attempting to write while licking my seeping, festering wounds. I am frantically hoping they will heal. My heart is in shreds. My bank account is tapped. My psyche is pulverized. I have been attempting to climb a slimy, rickety ladder out of a very deep, dark hole. I'm exhausted. I'm tired of the unending rungs. They run above me into a dark, brutal, and fathomless sky.

I know I can't make it. I'm finished! I can barely walk. With each step, I gain a certain satisfaction on each and every one of my trips to the refrigerator, seeking a new soldier to kill. I know Leilauna was the one who pulled the trigger. I can see the gun in her hand, and her smile, that mischievous little smile I saw the first time I laid eyes on her, when she had looked over her shoulder at me, the day she had wrangled my very soul.

Women I have met and seen on the street and then went out with, all have paled beside my memories of Leilauna. She had strummed my chords just so. And so, no one could strike them like her. She was something...she had been astounding, while she favored me. She had been an experience, for lack of more appropriate words. An experience, I finally realized, I would likely never get over.

I was drinking more than heavily again. I just didn't feel like turning it off. I was thinking *What the hell!* I was reveling in *my* misery. It was a state of suffering I had earned. It was *all* my own, and by God I was going to run its treacherous gauntlet to the freaking dismal end!

My writing took a downturn...and then I couldn't write at all. It *had* turned up. The evidence that is...it's name was Leilauna. For *that* miracle to work its magic, I was forced into signing away everything I owned, except for my condo. They didn't want the condo—not enough equity, too hard to manage at a distance, etc., so I was spared my meager personal belongings and the safe space of a roof over my head. I had nothing else but the promise of two books to be completed, and the deadlines were either past due or staring me straight in my broke ass, writer's blocked face. I was miserable and un-consolable. Insufferable misery had become my master. I reveled in the feeling of being no longer in control of my destiny. She had stolen that belief from me. She had stolen much more than that, and with each beer I swilled, the list of her thefts grew larger.

Well, I *could* write, but all that ever flowed from my disheveled mind onto the page was a tear-soaked, beer-stained rambling account of the tenderness that had turned into unbelievable and insufferable torment.

I had received the check sent by my editor as an advance on the book. I was locked up on the title…I had thought of a thousand titles, but none of them were right. None of them caught the moment…or I should say "moments,"—all sixteen vicious months of weeks running down to days that broke my mind into deciphering hours and ultimately the minutes I had been wrongfully incarcerated for a crime that was no crime at all.

The nothing on the page struck me as special. Drinking became my distraction. The most important substance became the cold one in my hand. When I had nothing better to do, I could try and remember where I had left my last open one. *That* kept me busy. When it couldn't easily be found, I would throw caution to the winds and open another.

WHAT TITLE could convey all that?

I drank *in* my unhappiness. I drank *in* my sorrow. I reveled in the shambles of my finances. I was slowly wandering down a dark road—a road few return from, a road that led most people into oblivion. The fact was this: I just didn't care anymore. I had laid out a brand new, as yet un-tread doormat for oblivion to wipe its determined feet upon. I was welcoming oblivion!

She had broken me. That Wretched Bitch! Leilauna had broken me! The thought spiked into my heart. I staggered to the refrigerator and opened another.

Somewhere between the refrigerator and my way back to the couch, I passed out.

Chapter 50

I WOKE IN a pool of dried beer and broken glass. I had severed nothing strategic. The minor cuts had clotted and stopped bleeding before my miserable life's blood had oozed completely away.

I was more depressed than ever.

I could never be brave enough, I thought in desperation, to put a gun against my head and pull the trigger. I could never just step out in front of a rushing beer truck and end my suffering by being splattered into a human Slushie. I *could* hope to pass out into a pile of broken brown glass and wasted beer, and end a life that seemed to be no longer worth living while blacked out and feeling absolutely no pain at all.

My life, if you could call it a life, went on in that way. It seemed to be dragging into months, but it had been less than three weeks. I began to pen notes, many of them in my drunken stupors. The fleeting months of the game Leilauna had played with my tender soul began taking shape. The game I had lost without realizing I had been playing one. John had originally said I was "playing with fire." In sober moments, I formulated the notes—my broken, tattered, beer-stained notes—into a rambling account of her wiles, her strategy, her enjoyment, her absolute dominion over me, while she deftly planned the ruination of my life.

Attempting to extricate myself from her bondage, I wrote. At first, it was a quick escape. Then, as the situation became more tenuous, it became my refuge, my hiding place, my safe haven from an ever-brewing storm when she was near me in the haunting memories that ever plagued my beleaguered mind..

And so, set before you in these abbreviated pages, for the reader of this journal, is my story—the actual account of my decent from heaven, life with the woman of my dreams, to hell...life without her.

Now I see only darkness.

She's gone, and mostly I wish she wasn't.

I most often wish, sickly, that I was in her temporal and heavenly clutches one more time—one more time that I could hold onto in my memory until my dying day.

That is how badly I miss her.

Something had to change, I thought. But I had no willpower left. I had no desire, no gumption. I had been swept up into the ocean of alcoholic losers. I reveled in drifting away.

I would wake in the morning. Or was it afternoon? It really didn't matter anymore. I would wake up and do the one thing that made me feel better. I would walk the beach.

For some reason, I really liked the massive, sun-bleached driftwood log that Leilauna and I had sat upon so many times during her visit to Seattle. It was just down the beach from my condo. So many logs came and went. This one was anchored. For as long I had lived here, it had been a landmark to this beach. It had been washed up by the winds of a winter storm and an extreme high tide. There would have to be a massive and catastrophic event in nature's golden realm to steal this grounding rod from me.

I reveled in its comfort. I walked the sand daily. I sat on it often. The log was my trusted old friend. It was solid. It would be there for me, no matter how I felt.

Sometimes I would sit there for hours, reviewing the shattered pieces of my life. Pieces that were strewn so far from one another that I held no hope of gluing them back into any semblance of my former self.

I just liked to sit there and watch the water and the birds.

Often times, I would think of her. I would see a woman that had a similar shape or mannerism...my mind would want to believe it was her. I chalked it up to being a *very* screwed up mess.

One evening, I was about to pry my ass away from the giant driftwood log and shuffle home to my refrigerator, and the dozen old friends that waited for me within, when....

A familiar voice sounded in my mind.

"Marry me, Jay."

The voice was a knife to the heart. It had sounded so real...in the haze that permeated my thinking, I had almost believed it was *her* voice instead of the memory of it.

Then I saw a shadow next to me on the log. It had long, wavy hair in which the gentle breeze played. The shadow got bigger, and she was there, sitting next to me, facing the opposite direction. We were side to side—me facing the water and her, the street.

I was speechless. Anger began to flood my mind. But her voice calmed me, and I gave her the last shred of patience I owned. I listened to the voice I had missed *so* desperately. The voice I had *once* loved.

"The last time we sat here," she began, "I said I didn't want to play hardball. Do you remember?"

I nodded. "Yes."

"I also said either way that I would have what I wanted. Do you remember?"

"Yes!" I said. "I remember. You got what you wanted. Now why don't you leave me the *fuck* alone?"

I had nearly screamed the words. It had been a tremendous effort to keep my volume low, not to lash out.

"But I haven't, Jay."

"Haven't *what*?" I asked, incredulous that she could be *here*, in my neighborhood, taunting me.

"I haven't gotten what I wanted."

She looked into me. I saw the flashing colors in her eyes again. The electric energy caught me up, and I tingled all over.

"Jay...marry me...that's all I wanted...all I *still* want!"

She moved in and pecked my cheek like she had done the first time when we had been swimming in the dynamite hole.

I blinked in disbelief.

She came in again, pressing her lips tight to mine.

My heart was pounding...I was dreaming again...of the tenderness...of the...of the places she had taken me...of our journeys within an unbelievable world of joy. It was a world I had never experienced before meeting her—a world to which I longed to return.

I was thinking that it couldn't *possibly* be true.

She must have seen the disbelief in my eyes and said, "Yes, Jay...it's true. It is time. All I ever wanted was you. But *only* as my husband."

Speechless, I nodded ever so slightly. Words were out of the question. The tangled thoughts jumping back and forth inside my head would have only slipped from my mouth, like three feet of melting snow, sliding and crashing down from a very steep steel roof.

My vision blurred. Nearly everything was completely out of focus. I could only see her. Something caught in my chest, and I felt a weak tremble down there, a tremble that grew into something like a shudder when I'm really cold.

Leilauna's wonderfully familiar and stunningly gorgeous features engulfed me. In the absence of words, I could hear the breeze bringing soft waves upon the beach. A seagull cried its familiar forlorn music. Her black, wavy hair fluttered, as it had so many times in my haunting memories.

She took hold of my hand and stood. I was powerless to do anything but silently move with her. As we walked, she said lightheartedly, "Let's go pack your things. I have two first class tickets for a flight tomorrow morning to Mussel Shoals."

"Don't you think Big John would be a perfect choice as your best man?"

I just nodded, and walked beside her in awestruck silence. Our shoes pressing into the sand were the most important thing in the world. Our footprints, side by side, were all that mattered.

Then she said, "Don't forget, you promised Ben to help find his daughter, Zurie. By the way, I don't know if Ben told you…but, she's my mother.

CPSIA information can be obtained at www.ICGtesting.com
Printed in the USA
BVOW071144270113

311619BV00002B/24/P